ROYAL GHOULS

A Greek Ghouls Mystery

ALEX A. KING

For my sister, who likes this series. She is a woman of good taste.

CHAPTER ONE

THE WOMAN WAS POISED on cliff's sharp edge, threatening to jump from Merope's highest point. A disturbing distance below, the Aegean Sea was slapping itself into a frenzy against the island's rocks. The month was October—the cold end of October—but she was dressed for an August that happened twenty years ago. The jumper didn't have a name, not one she was willing to give me, anyway. She wore Jennifer Aniston's "Rachel" 'do and lashings of matte lipstick, waist-high Levi's 501s and something skimpy that was supposed to be a top.

"Say something," she said. "Stop me if you can."

Further along the cliff's edge, I was lying on my belly, staring down the twin barrels of binoculars. I didn't look up. This was the tenth time in the past hour that she had leaped to her death. For years, she'd been making the same jump. Ever since my family moved to Merope.

"No. Don't. Stop."

My name is Allie—"Aliki" if you're my mother and I'm in trouble—Callas and I see dead people. In my experience ghosts aren't spooky. Mostly they specialize in Too Much Information, and if I had to stick an adjective to them, I'd pick "annoying."' When I'm not seeing dead people—and when I am—I run Finders Keepers, a business dedicated to finding things for people. Sometimes the job is hunting down missing people. Other times it's information or an impossible-to-find knick-knack for that special someone. I'm the first stop when that cheating jerk is planning to rip you off and you need proof before you hire someone else for the revenge part. My job means I'm a magnet for useless and useful information. Sooner or later, everything reaches my ears. People with secrets—especially other people's secrets—can't help sharing. I'm thirty-one, single, and when my parents get back from their round-the-world cruise, it's possible they'll bring presents for my sister and her family and an international assortment of men for me.

"Nobody will save me. Everybody hates me."

"I guess you'll go eat worms?"

The ghost turned around, questions all over her face. "Eh?"

My American roots were showing. The product of two Greek-Americans, I'd moved to the island paradise of Merope at the age of thirteen, when my parents finally caved, after years of familial manipulation. There's only so much "your insert-random-relative is dying—again!" a person can take without cracking up or moving back to Greece. My parents are emotionally stable, so they crammed everything into suitcases and dragged us across the Atlantic Ocean.

"Never mind," I said. "I'm trying to work here, so whatever you need to do, do it quietly."

The jumper sighed like I was killing her, then fell. Her non-corporeal body jerked as it soundlessly hit every rock on the way down, then landed in the Aegean Sea's cooling waters.

I started to count. "One ... two ... three ... and ..."

"Say something. Stop me!"

She was back, dressed head to toe in the same outfit. It was dry and so was she.

"Okay."

"You are not going to say anything?"

"Nice weather we're having."

October is one of Greece's kindest months. Skin doesn't blister the way it does in July, and winter hasn't spanked the land with its cold wooden spoon. This afternoon, the sky was a cloudless blue, and I had barely shivered at all since I peddled my bicycle to the sharp edge of Merope.

"That is all?" Hands on hips. "You want to talk about the weather?"

"Trying to work here."

"Who works on the edge of a cliff?"

"Don't you have to jump to your death again?"

"Rude," she said, and took a flying leap.

One ... two ... three ...

"What are you doing up here?" she asked me.

"I find things people can't or don't want to find on their own. Sometimes it's stuff, sometimes it's information, sometimes it's other people. Today it's a boat."

"Oh," she said. "What's on the boat?"

"A man."

Suddenly we weren't alone on the cliff. A barrel-shaped ginger cat appeared. He had an overbite and he looked pissed off at the entire world. But he seemed to like me enough to keep coming back for more of whatever it was that attracted him to me in the first place. Dead Cat was dead and had been for decades. And now he was my dead cat, thanks to someone who had meant the world to me.

"Awww, a cat!" The ghost woman crouched down, wiggled her fingers. "I used to love cats. I had a cat once, until it tried to tackle a donkey."

Dead Cat sat his hefty rump down not far from the

woman and looked her up and down. The wicked glint in his eye said this was a giant mouse and he was determined to drag it home and abandon it on my doormat.

"Don't even think about it," I hissed.

The inherited cat turned around in a circle, then stood with his hindquarters facing the dead woman. My Virgin Mary, was he going to spray her? He'd done it before with a living woman and she hadn't felt a thing.

Dead Cat's back paw shot out, nailed her in the calf.

"*Gamo tin mana sou* ..." the woman howled as she toppled off the cliff again, suggesting that I make sweet love to my mother. Even in Ancient Greece that was frowned upon. There was a whole myth about the dangers of nookie with your own parent.

I gave my dead cat a mock exasperated look. "You're incorrigible."

He ratcheted his purr up to steam train.

"Now I'm falling when I'm not supposed to," the ghost woman said, reappearing. "Being dead is frustrating. I was hoping for more."

"There's a whole organization for dead people in the Afterlife. You should check it out."

She shot me an interested look. "An organization? What kind of organization?"

"One that helps people transition and cope with their new situation. It's called the Council of the Formerly Living."

"How do I get there?"

"I don't know," I said. "I'm still alive."

"Now you are just bragging." She fell again.

For the next four seconds I focused on the sea.

I had told the ghost I was waiting on a boat, which was true. Angela Zouboulaki, my perennial client, had recently embarked on a new manhunt. She'd never met the man in question. Normally Angela hunts in meatspace, but this time she'd lined up a new boyfriend online. Johnny Margas was sailing into port this afternoon on a yacht named the Sand Witch, and my task was to snap pictures of the man in question, shooting them to Angela before he showed up on her doorstep. She wanted to make sure he was everything he said he was, visually speaking. Men are potato chips to Angela: she can't eat just one. She had started life dirt poor but married her way to the top of Greece's financial food chain, confiscating assets from one dead husband and one ex.

So far there wasn't any sign of her imminent lover boy, but there were several promising blips on the horizon.

Four seconds was up. The ghost popped back.

"What can you tell me? Anything useful?"

"Not much. I don't know how to access the Afterlife or the Council. My impression is that you don't have a choice. You're sort of collected. Have you seen the light yet?"

"No, just water. I cannot seem to stop jumping."

"Have you tried?"

"No! I wish I had thought of that."

The sarcasm was strong with this one. "Any idea why?"

"No." Her foot stuck out again, as though she was about to jump. Then she stopped. "There's a yacht," she said. "Maybe it's your man."

One of the distant dots had broken away from the pack and was floating this way. Hopefully it would be Angela's beau, and hopefully he would be everything he said he was. Don't get me wrong, Angela's money was nice, especially in my bank account, but she was addicted to deadbeats and in dire need of an intervention.

I twiddled the dial. Focused. Big yacht. Fancy. Expensive. Somebody who was somebody owned this yacht. Maybe Angela's third ship really was coming in.

"Maybe," I murmured.

The dead woman plunged into the sea again.

One ... two ... three ...

"That boat is moving fast," she said. "And I know because I see a lot of boats from up here."

She was right. The yacht was coming in fast—too fast.

Refocus.

Seven people on the deck. Five bikini-clad brunettes. Beautiful, bronzed women whose job it was to look pretty. The kind who came to the island all the time to shop and complain. One elderly man, six months pregnant, the kind of deep mahogany tan that made dermatologists twitch. King of all he surveyed. A sixth woman with a smooth face that reminded me of canvas stretched in an embroidery hoop. She was sixty faking fifty. They were your average seafaring tourists.

The dead woman crossed herself frantically. "Stop them!"

"I can't. It's too late."

"You have to do something!"

"Did you miss the part where I said I can't?"

The yacht's passengers suddenly noticed Merope's cliff face staring them down. They jumped up and down, arms waving, screaming in the seconds before the yacht collided with the island and lost the world's most epic game of rock, fiberglass, engine parts. None of them jumped overboard. It would have been pointless anyway. They were already dead, and had been long before the boat ran headfirst into Merope.

Not the yacht, though. That was real, and now it was burning.

———

Every law enforcement officer on Merope was leaning over the edge of the cliff, watching the yacht burn. Down in the water, emergency workers and local fishermen were dousing the flames from their boats. Lots of yelling. Creaking, groaning metal. One of the fishermen was using this opportunity to grab lunch. Using a fishing spear as a stick, he was cooking a fish in the flames.

"This fire is making me hungry," Constable Pappas said, eyeing the fish. Gus Pappas is a rookie cop. He looks like a good, hard sneeze could knock him over. He has hair but you wouldn't know it because he attacks his head with a razor every chance he gets.

"Pappas?" I said.

"What?"

"There is something seriously wrong with you."

"Why?"

I shook my head. "Never mind."

"I have to make jokes," he said, "otherwise I will vomit." The blood drained out of his skin. A green tint took over.

"Are you okay?"

"I should not have thought about it."

He leaned over and projectile puked off the cliff. I handed him a tissue. He used it to wipe his mouth, then he tossed the tissue over the cliff. I watched it waft down to the fire, where it was immediately gobbled up.

"Sorry," Pappas said. "It's my first disaster."

It was mine, too, but my stomach chose its own protests and it didn't seem to mind this too much.

A short distance away from Constable Pappas, Detective Leo Samaras was watching the whole thing unfold, ear pressed to his phone. His handsome face was grim. Leo is a hundred and ninety centimeters (six feet, two inches) of solid muscle and pale caramel skin. His hair is dark and his eyes hover in that ethereal place between green and brown. The man knocks my socks off with his sex appeal ... and in the old days he was my sister's high school sweetheart. A couple of weeks ago, we went on our first and only date.

I didn't want talk about it. Now. Or ever.

As though he knew he was on my mind, Detective Samaras swiveled around to look at me.

"Body," he said.

I looked down. Was he missing an adjective?

"Thanks—I think."

His forehead crumpled like a napkin. He moved the phone away from his mouth. "What?"

"You said something about a body."

His gaze cut to Constable Pappas, who was looking less green and more white now. "They found a body on the boat." He frowned into his phone. "Two bodies. No survivors yet. It's a mess down there. There won't be anything left of the vessel at this rate. The Hull Identification Number is already gone."

"Would the name help?" I asked him.

"Better than nothing. Why? Did you see it?"

Behind him, the refugee from a 1990's sitcom fell all over again. *Pop!* And she was back again. She waved at me. Now wasn't a good time to wave back. Detective Samaras—Leo—already thought I was a kook with a thing for scaling out bathroom windows. Just because I wanted to avoid him for the rest of my life, didn't mean I wanted him to doubt my sanity.

I made eye contact with the ground. Parched dirt. Stones. Wisps of browning grass. "The Royal Pain. That's the yacht's name. English Alphabet."

He was staring at me, wasn't he? My eyes flicked up then back down. Yup, he was staring. Rude ... and also kind of hot. That was a problem. *He* was a problem.

"Sounds familiar," he said. "You know almost everything that happens around here. Does it sound familiar to you?"

"Vaguely."

"Any ideas?"

"None."

"Want to brainstorm together over bad food and worse drinks later?"

"No," I said. "But thanks."

I broke away from the pack, grabbed my bicycle, and kept on going.

———

Vasili Moustakas was shuffling down the main street, one slipper at a time. As always, his sausage was dangling through the hole in his pajamas, searching for fresh air. No one except me noticed old *Kyrios* Moustakas. ((*Kyrios* and *Kyria* are the Greek words for Mr. and Mrs. To be on the socially safe side, it's best to tack the correct one onto the front of everyone's first or last name, if they're from a generation older your own. Otherwise everyone will talk about you, and the talk will not be nice.) He had been killed a couple of months ago by a horny teenager with a fresh grudge against him and an old nose. The grudge was older now, but the teenager's nose was new—and so was her prison jumpsuit.

"Little Aliki Callas," he called out.

Greece is a country wrapped up in social protocols. Ignore someone's greeting—especially an elder—at your own peril. Good people have become social pariahs after failing to say hello to an old widow with a big mouth and a desiccated fig for a heart. So the Greek blood that ran through my veins was okay with me waving to *Kyrios* Moustakas and wishing him a *kalispera*—good afternoon. Being considered crazy was far more socially acceptable than being rude.

He waved me over. "Come over here."

"Are you going to show me your *poutsa?*

He grinned. His rack of teeth had a lot of vacancies. "How did you know?"

I shook my head. "*Kalispera*, *Kyrios* Moustakas." I pushed away from the ground, preparing to ride off into the sunset.

"Aliki Callas!"

I stopped. "What?"

"Have you got a cigarette?"

"I don't smoke."

"Too bad. I could really use a cigarette."

"They don't have cigarettes in the Afterlife?"

"They do not have a lot of things."

Like pajamas pants that fastened, obviously. Like most ghosts, Vasili Moustakas was wearing the outfit he'd died in, and he'd died in his pajamas. Not because the car struck him at night but because he wore the loose fitting pants everywhere, and had for decades. It's harder to be a flasher in regular pants. Zippers can bite; pajama pants just gum the sausage.

I didn't want to ask, but it had been that kind of day and my guard was down. Watching bodies burn will do that to a woman. "Like what?"

He shuffled over to where I was straddling my bicycle, wondering which of my limbs I would need to chew off to escape. Both legs were required for peddling, but what did I really need my left arm for anyway?

Kyrios Vasili widened his original grin. "The dead do not have an advocate in this world."

My mind boggled. "Why would dead people need an advocate here?"

"I slept with your *yiayia*, did you know that?"

Every time. Every damn time I got roped into a conversation with Kyrios Vasili, he circled back to his time in my grandmother's pants. When it came to Yiayia, he wasn't anything special. Half of Merope—male and (rumor had it) female—had taken a recuperative mini-break between her legs.

"It never came up in conversation."

"You know what came up during our conversation?"

"What?"

He pointed down at his pajama pants.

"I doubt if that has popped up in the past twenty years!"

I pushed away from the ground and zipped off towards home, leaving the grumbling ghost behind me, halfheartedly shaking his fist.

Home to twenty thousand people and change, Merope is one of the Aegean Sea's smaller jewels. I wouldn't call it home, but on days when I'm not PMSing I'd call it home-ish. You've seen Merope or a Greek island just like it on calendars, Pinterest, and Instagram. People want to come here but most of them never do. The climate is furnace hot in summer with a dash of mild winter. Sometimes we get a sprinkling of snow. We always get sin. Merope is Mykonos and Athens on cheap steroids, cut with grime and smut. But Merope doesn't lift its summer skirt and flash that at the tourists. No, the island saves its baggage for the locals.

On the way home I stopped at the More Super Market, one of two grocery stores close to my apartment. The Super Super Market is bigger and brighter, but I haven't stepped inside since my fiancé Andreas abandoned me while I was ordering cheese at the deli counter. I can't even look at the Super Super Market. Even riding past punches a new hole in my gut.

The More Super Market is the birthplace of salmonella. Dusty and dim, it is home to a host of pets. If rats and spiders are your thing, the More Super Market is for you. If you're a pervert, I hear they're hiring at the deli. And don't touched the bagged candy.

I bought groceries as I needed them. Lately, I was on a sandwich kick. My American roots were asserting themselves. I can cook—I do cook—but since my neighbor and best friend was murdered, I hadn't been the mood to whip up anything more complicated than sandwiches.

Peanut butter and grape jelly weren't staples on the More Super Market's shelves, so I made do with *kaseri* cheese, salami, and a jumbo jar of Merenda, Greece's version of Nutella. The More Super Market wasn't big enough for a conveyor belt, so I dumped my sandwich fixings on the single counter and prepared to defend my purchases.

"What are you going to make with those?"

Stephanie Dola, the store's teenage checkout chick and high school dropout, flicked her buck teeth with her chipped manicure. If Stephanie was a knife in a drawer full of spoons, she wouldn't be the sharpest object.

"Sandwiches."

"Sandwiches?"

"Two pieces of bread with cheese and meat in between."

"And the Merenda?"

"Dessert sandwiches."

"Dessert sandwiches?"

"Two pieces of bread, with Merenda in between."

"That's the strangest thing I've ever heard. Bagged chocolate is on sale this—"

"No thanks," I said quickly. Stephanie was too busy picking her teeth to pack my things so I shoved everything into the bag that held most of my professional life. "Did you hear a yacht crashed in to the island today?"

Fingers still in her mouth, Stephanie tilted her chin up then down. That little head tilt was what Greeks did instead of shaking their heads.

"So far they've found two bodies."

She pulled her fingers out of her mouth to change the subject. "I heard *Kyria* Marouli's granddaughter is going to be a movie." She looked left. She looked right. She leaned forward. "A porn movie."

"A porn movie?" The details were right-ish but the players were muddled up. Olga Marouli, my recently deceased neighbor and best friend, did have a granddaughter of dubious morality. But porn? That was the bailiwick of Jimmy Kontos, Merope's only little person and Detective Leo Samaras's cousin.

At least I didn't think Lydia would be involved. Not that it was any of my business. I'm a live and let live person, provided no one is trying to kill me or mine.

"That is what I heard."

"Probably you heard wrong."

She went back to picking her teeth. "Do you think you could ask her and find out?"

I felt my eyes bug. "You want me to find out if Lydia is doing porn?"

Stephanie's gaze did another sweep of the store. We were alone in the More Super Market.

"I could use the money," she said.

"You want to *do* porn?"

"Forget it," she said.

"You work a lot of hours. Aren't the Triantafillou brothers paying you for them?"

"They said because I'm still a teenager they don't have to pay me as much. Don't tell anyone I said anything," she pleaded.

"There are laws—labor laws. You're entitled to a fair pay rate and time off."

She brightened up. "Really?"

I swore I was telling her the truth and scored a relieved smile in return.

"I will talk to them," she said.

Kalispera, Stephanie," I said, wishing her a good afternoon. I grabbed my things and scrammed.

My apartment building sits a couple of rough blocks and

twists down the road. Like almost every residence on Merope, it is white. Three floors, six apartments, one fountain in the courtyard, and a garden that is tended to by the ghost of a former gardener. Of course, most ghosts can't affect the world around them, so a real gardener swings by regularly to pick up his slack.

Recently I discovered that my best friend and neighbor was also my landlord. After her murder, when it was time for all her worldly goods to be divvied up, she left apartment 202 to me.

And that's how I became a homeowner.

I would return it in a heartbeat if I could have Olga Marouli back.

———

As if the number doesn't give it away, my apartment is on the second floor. The apartment across the hall—and the rest of the building, except for 202—belong to Lydia Marouli, Olga's granddaughter. Today German pop music was creeping under her front door and making a run for it. So far Lydia was a good neighbor. Sometimes we passed in the hallway and exchanged smiles. Occasionally, just to mix things up, we threw words into air between us. Small words without meaning. It was really working for us.

This evening the only sign of Lydia was her music, and even that would be gone once I was contained within the protective shell of my apartment.

I unlocked the door and stepped inside.

Then I turned around and walked back out to give myself a moment.

And then I went back in.

Someone was in my apartment.

Wrong. Someones—plural. And they were having too

much fun with my dead cat, who was on his back, sucking up as much attention as he could get.

"I don't feed you, and this is how you repay me?"

The overgrown, and very dead, marmalade cat closed his eyes. If he couldn't see me, my disapproval didn't exist.

Asking my unwelcome and uninvited guests who they were was pointless. I already knew.

Not long ago, I had watched them crash into the side of Merope.

CHAPTER TWO

"Look at me," I said. "Do I look like a policewoman?"

The answer to that question was no. No, I did not look like any kind of person in law enforcement. If you want to get American about it, I'm five-seven (or 1.70 centimeters). My hair is long, dark, and was currently caught up in a claw clip. Fashionable, no. Practical, sometimes, when it wasn't biting into my scalp. My eyes are dark and intense, beautiful, piercing, poop-colored, and "Oh God, is that pink eye?" depending on who you ask. I call them brown. Okay, so my wardrobe's color of choice these days was black, but there was nothing cop-like about me.

The group's mouthpiece scraped his gaze up and down, from boots to hoodie. To his credit, he didn't hold up a score card and rank me out of ten. "A policewoman can look like anything, especially if they are undercover."

"You want a cop?" I pointed at my ceiling. "Detective Samaras lives upstairs. He's dragging your bodies out of the water right now, but he'll be home sooner or later."

"If I wanted a policeman I would go to the police. What I need is someone who can solve my murder."

Me, me, me. I, I, I.

I had a feeling he was a recurring theme in his life. The dead man even dressed the part of the self-absorbed control freak. Captain's hat. Navy blue blazer with gold buttons. White pleated slacks, for that impregnated-six-months-ago look that plagued men of a certain age and lifestyle. He looked like the kind of man who paid a hundred euros for a steak, then smothered it in ketchup.

The thing about ghosts is that, with a few exceptions, they're annoying. Somewhere between here and there they lose filters. Parts of their personalities are distilled—and not always the pleasant parts. Even Kyria Olga had been a blindingly bright shade of her former self as an apparition. So maybe I'd misjudged the man. Could be he used to be a sweet and polite, the human equivalent of a golden retriever. Here and now, the late-sixties man was already a pain.

The rest of his entourage was what you'd expect. Lots of barely-there bikinis and oversized sunglasses. Their religion was Kardashian and their budget was billionaire. Dark hair. Same builds. Their features came from the same surgeon or the same DNA. The dead man's daughters, maybe?

There was only one standout in the crowd of seven, and she did it by being fully clothed. Fake Captain's wife, perhaps? The two of them were located in the same decade—the sixth one—although maybe at opposite ends. She had big blond hair, and red lipstick that was migrating to the rest of her face, using the thin lines radiating out from her lips as tiny rivers. She had chosen a loose sheath dress to die in. Scoop neck. No sleeves. Cream with blue accents. Her jewelry was too big for her bird-like frame.

Wallis Simpson was speaking out of her pancake butt when she said you couldn't be too rich or too thin.

"I don't solve murders," I said.

Not for any old person, anyway. Kyria Olga was different.

The septuagenarian had been my best friend in this whole world. Also, she'd nagged me in to accepting the job, so I had a choice between solving her murder or listening to umpteenth rounds of Tzeni Vanou's *S'Agapo*. (In life and death, Olga Marouli had a thing for love stories, including *Ghost*. She believed repetition got results.)

"That is not what I heard."

"You heard wrong."

He pulled a business card out of thin air. One of my Finder Keepers business cards. Not *American Psycho* quality, but tasteful enough. It's hard to go wrong with black on white.

"Do you find things, yes or no?"

"Where did you get that?" I went to grab it but it wasn't there. Not in any physical sense, anyway.

"Message board."

My eyes narrowed. My body shuddered. Somewhere, a socially awkward and hungry tiger was pussyfooting over my grave. "Message board ... where?"

"In the Afterlife."

"You were in the Afterlife and you came back?"

"He had unfinished business, and he hates unfinished business."

Finally someone else in the group had spoken up: one of women I had decided were the yacht owner's daughters. She had been tussling with a straightening iron and won; every hair on her head was a limp stick. I couldn't pin an age to her, but if I had to guess I'd say somewhere between sixteen and twenty-five. It didn't matter really; in about thirty years, if she kept worshiping at the altar of the sun gods, she'd have the complexion of a leather sofa. No. Wait. She was dead. Sofa-skin averted.

"Unfinished business?" I asked.

"My murder," the father-in-question said.

The oldest woman, the one in the sheath dress, glanced around my apartment. "I cannot believe people live like this."

My apartment wasn't much but it wasn't tragic. The bones were excellent and maintenance worked on regular time, not Greek time. Greek time can be roughly translated as "whatever, whenever".

I raised my hand. "*People* are here, you know."

The maneuver was completely unnecessary, but I opened my front door anyway. Walls were not normally an obstacle for the dead.

"Okay, time to go. All of you." One of the bikini bimbos picked up Dead Cat. He didn't seem too offended. "Except the cat. The cat stays."

The captain and his entourage look at each other, puzzled expression on their faces—what I could see if their faces anyway; those sunglasses were massive.

My Virgin Mary, what now? "Is there a problem?"

"No—no problem." He stood there, stuck on stupid. They all did.

"There *is* a problem. I can tell."

He popped his cuffs with those heavy gold buttons. "How do we leave?"

"You came here, remember? Do that, but in reverse."

"You are not very helpful."

"And you are still here, in my apartment."

The dead man strode over to the living room window, where the view was currently limited to a smattering of lights. Arms behind his back, he stared into what he believed was the sea but was actually late evening gloom over a parking lot.

Oh, no, no, no. *Not* okay.

"The door is that way." I pointed to the emergency exit, AKA: the door hole, in case death was messing with his vision.

He didn't turn around. "Normally I would fire an

employee as unmotivated and unambitious as you, but because I am dead and I need your help, I am willing to be lenient and give you an opportunity to prove yourself."

This guy was a piece of work.

Greeks have a word that covers a dizzying array of personality flaws: *malakas*. Taken literally, it means someone has devoted so much time to spanking the monkey that their brain has softened to mush. His brain wasn't mush (he no longer had a brain) but the word still applied.

"I don't want to prove myself. I'm going to sit over there" I nodded to my desk "and work on cases that aren't yours. Then, if you're not gone, I'm going to buy some sage and wave it about until you leave. Your death—"

"Murder."

"—is a police matter, and the police aren't fans of outside interference."

"I have a list of suspects you can give to them."

Against my better judgement, my inner feline perked. All Greek DNA comes with a bonus cat hair. "You have suspects?"

He whipped a sheet of paper out of thin air. "Take this."

The paper wafted to the ground. I couldn't pick it up because it was ghost paper. Every time I tried it slipped through my fingers.

The scantily clad peanut gallery giggled.

My sigh was big and loud and clearly said that they were a major pain in several of my vital organs. "Give me a list and I'll give it to the police. Afterwards, you float away and leave me alone. Deal?"

He stuck out his hand. I couldn't do a thing with it except stare.

"I do not like being dead," he said, returning the hand to its position behind his back. "I am finding it inconvenient."

The older woman who had opened her mouth to criticize my apartment opened her mouth again. "I have questions. Can we change clothes? Because I do not want to spend eternity in this old thing."

The answer to her question was "yes." Too bad I wasn't in an accommodating mood. Not after she had insulted my place—my place that she had chosen to infest.

"If you would hop on your broom and whizz back to the Afterlife you'd find out. They have orientation, the Council for the Formerly Living, and all the help the newly dead require," I said in a huff.

Normally the dead don't come back for forty days. That's how long it takes to process their souls or some such thing. The Greek Orthodox church believes that the deceased use these forty days to visit their loved ones before jetting off to the big taverna in the sky. But in my experience they've got it backwards. First the taverna, then the visiting.

Exceptions exist. Kyria Olga bounced right back like a boomerang after her murder. Apparently the rules are stretchy and bendy when there's unfinished business like murder involved. At the time I thought I was going nuts, seeing someone who shouldn't be there, alive or dead.

"Just out of curiosity, when did you die?" I asked.

"I was murdered," the dead man said, tone indignant and superior.

Virgin Mary save me from nitpicking ghosts.

"Okay. When were you murdered?"

"This morning."

Laptop on. New document open. "Okay, give me the suspects' names."

Ten minutes later I had a list of names. "Who are these people?"

The dead man was all too happy to puff up his shoulders

and tell me. "Envious people. Former business partners. Politicians."

"What did you do? When you were alive, I mean." Alive, as recently as this morning.

"I was bread."

"I don't understand."

He sighed like my intellect was in the low double digits. "Royal Pain."

"Your yacht?"

"My business."

A light came on in my head. Not a giant glowing ball of radiance; more like an LED nightlight in a closet. "Not pain —*pain*. The French word for bread, not the English word for, well, pain."

"I cannot believe you are the best I can do," he muttered. "Yes, I am Harry Vasilikos and I own the Royal Pain bakery. As you cleverly deduced, Pain is French for bread and Royal is English for Vasilikos."

Royal Pain. I'd heard of it. The sliced bread had taken over supermarket shelves on the mainland years ago.

"We don't have that here," I said.

"It is just a matter of time until Royal Pain bread takes over Merope's bread market."

I laughed. "Newsflash: It was never going to catch on."

Merope is one of those places where old habits take longer to die than a cockroach during a nuclear winter. The island has residents who refuse to believe cars exist. They get around on foot and by donkey, and if a car almost hits them they insist it was a devil. Grubby hole-in-the-wall bakeries exist in every Merope neighborhood. On any day except Sunday, men, women, and children on Merope can buy a loaf of bread hot enough to burn the whorls and loops off their fingertips. Soft, pillowy loaves with crusty shells, leaking steam and that intoxicating fresh bread aroma. There was no way Royal Pain's plastic packages of sadness could compete with that.

"Also," I added helpfully, "you're dead. You are officially no longer selling bread."

"True, but I did not get to the top of the loaf by being a fool. I have contingency plans. The expansion of my business will go on."

Dead Cat was still blissed out with a half dozen bikini girls scratching his various cat-approved zones. One of Harry Vasilikos's daughters had wandered into my bedroom and was currently checking out my clothing situation, which was perfect for my job but not remotely suitable for Tweeting on a yacht. And *Kyria* Vasiliko, (the dropped "s" is not a typo; Greek women don't typically get an "s" at the end of their last names; I'm one of the exceptions), if that was her name, was staring into the void. From her expression I could only surmise that it was staring back. If any of these people knew about contingency plans, their faces weren't coughing up details.

"Well ... I don't really care," I said. "*Mi casa* not *su casa*. So I'm going to give this to the police, and then you can leave. I don't care how you do it. Use the door if you have to, like a regular person." I printed the list, snatched it off the printer, and left.

As luck (good or bad, it was hard to say) would have it, Detective Leo Samaras lived directly above me. Given today's tragedy, and the absence of footsteps above my head since I had arrived home, I knew his apartment was empty.

Perfect.

I jogged up to the third floor, folded the list of suspects in the Royal Pain murder, and slid it under 302's door.

Done. Go, me. Time to escape to the safety of my apartment and work on evicting the ghosts.

Behind me 302's door flew open, thwarting my getaway.

My heart jumped up into my throat. I launched myself at the steps and rolled, hitting the wall.

"You're crazy, you know that?" Jimmy Kontos said, shaking his head.

"Willow Ufgood, we have to find Madmartigan," I said, hauling myself up off the floor. "Otherwise Bavmorda will kill Elora Danan!"

Jimmy Kontos is more hair than man, all of it blond and wiry. He has big hair and a matching beard. Could be it's some kind of elaborate hair balaclava. Technically he's a dwarf, but that doesn't stop him from being an average-sized *malakas*. For artistic reasons, he changed his last name from Samaras to the Greek word for 'short.'

Merope's only little person, and Leo Samaras's cousin, looked me up and down. He put two fingers to his lips and whistled, loud and sharp. "Did anyone throw some magic beans out the window, because I've got a giant situation here."

I peered over his head. "Where's the chocolate?"

His forehead bunched up. "Chocolate?"

"This is Willy Wonka's factory, isn't it?"

He shut the door, then opened it again. He was holding the suspect list. "What is this?"

"A list of people who want to hear you sing the Munchkin Land song." I looked him over. Something about him seemed weird—weirder than usual.

"What are you wearing?"

"Ugg boots," he said, lifting up his feet, one at a time.

Sure enough, he was wearing sheepskin boots. No wonder I hadn't heard him padding around upstairs. On Jimmy the boots were knee-high.

"No, that's not it. Are you wearing makeup?"

His eyes narrowed. "What's wrong with makeup? You never seen an actor wearing makeup before?"

An actor. Ha. Jimmy Kontos was the lead performer in a series of skin flicks called *Tiny Men, Big Tools*.

"Not on Merope."

Merope is old-school. Men don't wear makeup or women's clothing unless it's Sunday and their wives are at church.

"But hey," I went on, "you do you."

"How did you know?"

I was lost. This conversation had spiraled out of control in one sentence. "Huh?"

"The makeup is for reshoots. I have to act out some solo closeups and send them to the director."

Horrible thoughts danced around my brain, Rockette style. Lots of high kicks. Every one of my mind's Rockettes had Jimmy's face and a tool belt. Also, for some inexplicable reason, they were wearing high-heeled Uggs, which I prayed would never become a thing.

Desperate to preserve what was left of my sanity and lunch, I pivoted on one heel and bolted.

"Careful, Fezzik," Jimmy hollered after me. "All that running, people might mistake you for an earthquake."

————

My apartment was empty when I barreled through the door, eager to escape the mental image of Jimmy Kontos working hard for the money.

No, wait, everyone was crammed into my bathroom, crowded around the mirror.

Great. Perfect.

"What are you doing?"

The gaggle of barely-dressed women-children giggled. "We're invisible."

"Like vampires," one of Harry Vasilikos's daughters said. The way she said it, I knew someone was a *Twilight* fan-girl.

"Are you leaving any time soon?"

"No," Harry Vasilikos said. He was standing in my shower, staring up at the sprayer. "It is hot in here. Why is it so hot in here? Have you solved my murder yet?"

"The heat is probably some kind of residual effect from the fire when your yacht crashed into the island."

"Really?"

"No idea," I said cheerfully. "I'm just making it up, hoping you get sick of me and leave. Maybe the Greek Orthodox Church is wrong and hell does exist. That heat you're feeling might be a portent of things to come."

"For a helpful person, you are not helpful."

"You promised to leave when I passed on that list of suspects."

"I already told you, I don't know how. First I was in a waiting room, then I was here. If you can talk to ghosts, I suggest you show some initiative and ask some of them how I can leave."

"Try the door."

Seven ghosts lined up at my front door. One at a time, they took a stab at leaving. One at a time, they were bounced back.

Harry Vasilikos peered down his leathery nose at me. "Even if I wanted to leave—and I do not, not until you find my murderer—I could not leave. In a way, I am as trapped as you are."

Kyrios Harry returned to the window. The dead women went back to my bathroom.

"Wrong," I said. "I'm not trapped at all. I can leave any time I want. In fact, I'm leaving right now."

I charged into the bedroom and stuffed my pajamas into a bag, then to the bathroom to get my toothbrush. Nobody moved, so I was forced to reach through a transparent rack of racks to grab my deodorant and toothbrush. "I'll be back in the morning. Be gone or I'm calling the Ghostbusters!"

Dead Cat gave me a woeful look.

"Not you," I said. "You're my ickle, bickle dead kitty cat."

"Where are you going?" Harry Vasilikos called out.

"Wherever I want, because I'm not dead."

CHAPTER THREE

My sister Toula is me but with bigger boobs and a couple of extra years on her odometer. She has two cute kids, a husband who can't get his own beer from the refrigerator, and she possibly considers Leo to be her sole property, even though they broke up more than a decade ago. She also has a spare couch, which is really just her regular couch but with me on it.

Halfway to her place—an easygoing, pothole-dotted ten minute bicycle ride away—I skidded to a stop, epiphany blooming in my mind. Goats flooded onto the dirt-packed road, prodded along by their goatherd. The goatherd was dead and so were his goats. I waited while the night congealed around me; one at a time, Merope was snuffing its lights. Riding through the dead is rude if you can see them, so I waited. The interruption didn't bother me. It gave me time to mull over the ghost situation in my apartment. The last thing I needed was for my apartment to become a regular drop-in point for the local ghost population. I didn't have answers, brochures, or travel tips. What I had was a business that thrived on the money of living people, and a penchant for long hours spent poring over the internet, hunting for the ungettable get.

I had to get rid of the Vasilikos clan. Why they couldn't *poof!* away like other ghosts, I didn't know, but I knew someone who might be willing to give them tips. Which is why I turned my bicycle around at the ghost goats and peddled toward Merope's main road.

On Merope's cobbled main road, Vasili Moustakas was crossing, just to get to the other side. Once he reached his goal, he crossed back over again, his desiccated *poutsa* flapping in the sea breeze. Occasionally he would stop in the middle of the street, waggle his withered wares, and yell, "Come and get me, you Turks!"

I parked my bicycle against a lamppost and waiting for the old man to shuffle back to my side of the street. Autumn had thrown its dark blanket over the island, and now that there was a bone-clacking chill in the air, most people had flocked home to light their fireplaces and complain about the impending winter. Their feet were already hurting. It would be the hardest winter yet. I'd heard it all before—every year, in fact. Greeks weren't Greeks unless they were complaining about their feet.

Kyrios Moustakas stopped at the curb. His face split in a wide gummy grin. "Little Aliki Callas, you are out late. There are monsters around." The shoulder-shaking way he laughed, anyone would think he had told the best joke ever.

I ignored the bit about monsters. If there were monsters they probably had eyes. And for everything with eyes I carried pepper spray.

"*Kyrios* Moustakas, you've always been known as a man who knows a lot of things. I bet even now you know a lot."

"More than I did before." He said it proudly, chest out. Well, as *out* as something sunken can get. "What do you want to know, Aliki? I will see if I can help."

"How do you ... you know ... *poof*." I added sounded effects and performed something dangerously closed to interpretive dance. Fortunately, the night was forgiving, with all its darkness and shadows and the absence of people.

Kyrios Moustakas gawked at me like my *baklava* was missing its nuts. "*Poof*? What is this *poof*?"

"*Poof*!" This time I limited my movements to arm-waving. "When ghosts disappear and go other places."

"Go other places? Where am I going to go, *vre*? After that girl hit me with her car, the bank took my house and my children took the rest. I have nowhere else to go, so I stay here, where I had the best times of my life. I spent my youth here, chasing girls, you know."

"So, you don't know how to *poof*?"

He and his walker turned around. At the speed of half-dry paint down a wall, he crossed the street. Once he'd reached his destination he turned back and met me at the curb.

"No *poof*."

"Could you maybe ask another ghost how they do it?"

"Come here," he said, grinning. "I want to show you something."

"Is it your *poutsa*?"

His grin fell. "How did you know?"

I ignored his penis, thanked him for his time, and got back on my bicycle.

Where to now?

Ghosts have a tendency to come and go. Most, once they've seen all the sights and done the whole peeping Tom thing for a few years or so, choose to move on permanently to the next phase of their existence, whatever that is. Fun, games, and shenanigans in the Afterlife, I assume. Some stick around for various reasons. True love. Spite. Or because, like *Kyrios* Moustakas, they feel like they've got nowhere else to go.

Most of the ghosts I've met in my life eventually moved on—and I've met a lot. According to my sister, I had a string of imaginary friends from the time I was tiny.

Not imaginary. Not friends, exactly. More like a slew of dead relatives. We tea partied together. They cheerfully pretended to eat my leaf-and-dirt sandwiches and drink my toilet water tea. When my parents discussed getting me some mental help, I flipped a switch and ditched the dead ancestors when other people were around.

Most people keep skeletons in their closet. With all the ghosts in my closet, there's no room for bones.

Kyrios Moustakas hadn't panned out, so who would know about getting from A to B when you're dead? There are ghosts sprinkled all over Merope. Because they can be annoying, I don't make a habit of making friends with them or letting them know I can see them, so I wanted to keep my options limited.

I rode back to the tip of Merope, where the Royal Pain had crashed hours earlier. Emergency workers were still toiling away down below, picking the yacht's bones apart, hunting for meat. The police had left dry land; they were on the police department's boat, observing the operation.

No problem. I wasn't here for them.

The dead woman was in her usual place, poised on the cliff's edge.

"What happens if I fall now?" she asked me as I whacked the bicycle's kickstand with my boot. "It's a mess down there. I don't want to fall into a mess."

"Can't you move along the edge a bit? That way you'd miss the yacht."

Hands on hips. "How about I tell you how to die, eh? How would you feel about that?"

"Newsflash: you're already dead. Every jump since the first one is a rerun."

"And they said life was strange. Death is stranger." She stared out to sea for a long moment. "Will I ever be able to stop falling?"

"You've stopped now, right?"

She made a face and went diving off the cliff all over again. A moment later she popped back in to position, clothes dry, hair neat.

"That!" I said. "That thing you do where you're down there and then you're back here again. How do you do that?"

Her face scrunched up. "The *poof!* thing?"

"Exactly. The *poof!* thing."

"I don't know. It just happens."

My shoulders slumped. And here I thought I was really on to something. I thought for sure the woman would know, but she was another dead end—pun unavoidable.

"I don't suppose you could zip on over to the Afterlife, grab a definitive how-to manual for me, and zip back here?"

I was a loon; her face said so. "Do you think I would be here if I could go to the Afterlife?"

"Merope is nice in summer. A lot of people swear they'll never leave. Maybe you're one of them."

"If I could leave I—"

She fell again.

My phone rang, banishing the woman to the backseat in my attention span. Angela Zouboulaki, the client who'd sent me to the cliff in the first place, was on the other end.

"Did you find him yet?"

"Not yet. You missed all the drama."

Her voice got sharp and point. "What drama?"

I told her about the yacht crash but not the dead cargo that was currently stashed in my apartment.

"Probably it was sabotage," she said. "Rich, successful people do not kill themselves unless there is an indictment for money laundering headed straight for them." There was a moment of silence. "What was the yacht called?"

When I told her, I heard her eyebrows fail to rise. Angela is one of Botox's devoted victims. "Harry Vasilikos is dead?"

I could neither confirm or deny without making myself look like I had one foot in the psych ward and the other on a squashed fig. "The police haven't released the victims names yet. Do you know him?"

Of course she did. Angela knew everyone who slept on a pile of money. She'd married two of them and collected their millions.

"I know the family. Harry is bread on the mainland and on the larger islands, you know."

I bit my tongue. I had questions ... and mixed emotions to go with them. Apart from shooing them out of my apartment, I had no business with Harry Vasilikos and his family. But that cat hair in my DNA was wiggling again.

"Interesting," I said. Something was tickling the box in my brain where I stored random useless information. "You didn't marry him, did you?"

"Of course not. His lifespan would have been much shorter if we had married. You know how hard I am on husbands." It was true, her husbands had the longevity of pantyhose. Her second husband dropped dead just months after their divorce. "Now go, do that thing I pay you good money for, eh?"

"I'm on my way to the dock now to see if Johnny's boat showed up."

Technically I wasn't, but I could be. Now that I'd thought about it, the dock was a hotbed of ghost activity. Maybe one of the deceased denizens would be willing and able to help me with my *poofing* issues. Dead sailors and fishermen never leave the sea. Even when it's the sea that killed them they just make excuses for her behavior. "I was asking for it," is the most popular. They don't care that the Aegean Sea, like all large bodies of salty water, is a serial killer.

Coasting downhill on Merope was dangerous business, so I took it slow, alternating braking with dodging stones and the occasional lump of what I hoped was animal *kaka*, not human. When summer was done with the island, the waterfront businesses closed early, except for a few eateries the locals favored. Back on blacktop and concrete again, I sailed past Crusty Dimitri's and didn't make eye contact with the trio of rats scurrying along the sidewalk, away from the restaurant, which sells something that resembles pizza and souvlaki. Crusty Dimitri's meat is a mystery. The eatery is a shack with Medusa's head on the wall, two wobbly tables, and five chairs that will never match. I've heard there's a scoreboard on the kitchen wall to keep track of many people lose bowel control after a feed of souvlaki with random bacteria in the filling. Crusty Dimitri's owner is the local health inspector's brother, so nothing gets inspected. The only reason Crusty Dimitri's is open past summer is because they deliver. Why you would want toxic waste delivered to your home is beyond me, but I guess even the self loathing have to eat.

The dock was swathed in darkness, with a few lone puddles of pale yellow light from street lamps. A quartet of luxury vessels were tethered to moorings. Unlike the smaller fishing boats, they didn't bob. They sat heavy in the water, weighed down by golden bathroom fixtures and teak flooring. I moved from yacht to yacht, checking the names, hunting for Angela's latest potential mistake. No sign of the Sand Witch or Johnny Margas. He was running late, or not running at all.

Which left me free to go on a ghost hunt.

I wandered to the end of the dock and back again, wondering which of the salty ghost sailors and dock workers I should pick. The ghost sailors were gathered in loose packs, smoking ghost pipes, ghost smoke curling in the real night sky. The workers were hauling ghost cargo on and off ships and boats that weren't there. None of them paid attention to me. Being ignored by the living was their status quo.

I thought about opening with a seamen joke, but those don't translate well in Greek.

I approached the first cluster of dead fishermen. Heavy coats on a couple. Shirtsleeves on the men who'd drowned during summer. An overabundance of beards and other facial hair. A few familiar faces. Some of these men were lost at sea during my time on Merope. Their ghosts did what their bodies never could and returned home. When I greeted them, they gawked at me.

"Are you talking to us?" one of the older men asked. His eyebrows were high, partially tucked under his fisherman's hat.

I told them my name, told them I needed help.

"Callas ... Callas ..." another of the men said. They all made agreeable sounds that indicated they knew the name. Not surprising; my family had been here since this chunk of rock cut itself off the continent and shifted way offshore. He took a long puff of his pipe. "Now I remember. I knew your grandmother."

"Everybody knew my grandmother."

He chuckled. They all did. "We used to call her Olive Oil because she spread herself all over the place."

Using all my restraint, I prevented a sarcastic eye rolling. Nobody wants to hear about their grandmother's sexual shenanigans.

"Yes, yes, Yiayia slept with most of Merope. Wasn't that nice of her? She was a real philanthropist. All that sex was her version of *philotimo*." *Philotimo* is the most virtuous of Greek virtues. To simplify, it means doing nice stuff for others.

"Maybe you could pay her back for all that generous sex. For instance, right now her granddaughter—me—needs help."

"What can old, dead sailors do for a pretty girl who is still alive?"

"Why can't you Google?" a handlebar mustache with bloodshot eyes asked. "Google knows everything. That is what I have heard people saying."

"I figured I would ask the experts," I said.

"Experts in what?"

"Being dead. I need to know how you get around."

Pipes in mouths, they stared wistfully at the dark water. "How does any sailor travel? Always by sea."

"Even now that you're dead?"

"Now? We go nowhere." Their laughter was a gruff, gravelly chorus. Someone—several someones—had been yo-ho-hoing with a bottle of ghost rum. "This" he waved his pipe at the water "is paradise."

"So you don't go anywhere, you just stay here on the dock?"

He shrugged. They all did. "There is no reason to leave."

"What about when you want to go somewhere else?"

"Go somewhere else?" They exchanged puzzled glances. None of these guys had a clue what I was talking about. I thanked them for their time and wheeled my bicycle up to the main road again, wondering who to see next. If only Olga Marouli's ghost was still haunting me; she did *poofing* like a pro. My heart hurt thinking about my friend, and there was something in my eye. Probably it was allergies. I needed sugar and I needed it now before my blood sugar level dropped any lower.

And that's how I wound up outside the Cake Emporium, drooling. Betty Honeychurch's bakery had moved in to the long-vacant space around the time of Kyria Olga's murder. The regular window display had undergone a metamorphosis.

The midnight-colored curtain was still in place, but now it was the backdrop for a Halloween celebration. Candy pump-kins. Jack O Lantern cakes. Sugar spirits. Marzipan witches riding marzipan brooms with their marzipan cats.

Something wet dribbled down my chin.

Oh. That was me.

The door opened. A curl-besieged head poked out.

"You're right on time, luv," Betty Honeychurch said in her crisp English accent, eyes twinkling.

"Are you sure? It's late."

"It's never too late to eat cake or chat with friends."

Betty Honeychurch is ageless. Skin infant-smooth. Eyes that say she's been seeing everything there is to see since before the dinosaurs glimpsed the meteor headed right for them and said, "Is it a bird? Is it a plane? We don't know. Oh shit!" She dresses for comfort, and tonight she'd chosen the cozy pairing of flannel flamingo-patterned pajamas and a fuzzy robe. I wanted to be at home in flannel pajamas and a fuzzy robe. Alone. With no ghosts. Okay, Dead Cat could stay because I kind of liked the fur ball, and he didn't cost me a single euro in vet fees or food, but the others had to go.

"I meant to come earlier, but I got caught up in a thing ..." My brain and mouth trailed off. How do you adequately describe the scene of a nautical disaster, especially one that ends in a massive fireball?

Betty's curls bobbed as she nodded. "The yacht, I know. What a tragedy. I understand they've found six bodies so far. Those poor people. Are you all right?"

"They were already dead when the boat crashed."

"I know. That doesn't mean it wasn't awful to witness." Betty steered me to a comfortable sofa.

A sofa?

I looked around. The Cake Emporium's interior had undergone a transformation, much like the window display. It was all decked out for Halloween. Orange sofas and matching chairs, huddled around low tables shrouded in black table-cloths. Cabinets filled with sugar bats and spiders. Webs of spun sugar. Vampires of ... actually, the vampires looked real. They hovered in the dark corners, eyes glowing silver. Movie props, I told myself. Did Betty always go all out, decorating? As usual, the confectionary store had a split personality. One half sold sweets. The other displayed all kinds of woo-woo things. Ouija boards. Mysterious herbs and other unidentifi-able doodads. Crystal balls.

"I'm always redecorating," Betty said, answering my unasked question. "I can't help myself. Everything feels stale after a while, so next thing I know, I'm tossing out the old and hauling in the new. I just adore the holidays, don't you? Of course I know Greeks don't really celebrate Halloween, but that doesn't mean my customers and I can't."

She was right: Halloween isn't a Greek thing. We dress up like slutty nurses and half-naked superheroes in February before Lent, and we call it *Apokries*. Also, it goes for three weeks.

"I love it," I said truthfully.

"It reminds you of home? Sorry. The thoughts were just there for the plucking." Betty patted my hand and urged me to sit. Satisfied that I was comfortable, she quickly whipped up two steaming cups of hot chocolate and ferried them to the table, along with a candy pumpkin the size of two fists. She settled in the cozy chair opposite, tucking her feet up underneath her. "Tap the pumpkin with your spoon. Go on."

I picked up the spoon and gave the pumpkin a gentle tap. The shell cracked. A chunk of orange candy fell away, revealing a chocolate cake center.

"Wait until you get to the middle," she said. "Molten chocolate."

My spoon plunged into the cake. I took a bite. It was still warm.

"How?"

She leaned forward, eyes sparkling with delight. "Magic."

No doubt. Betty is anything but ordinary. For one, she's woo-woo herself. The tiny woman can read minds. She doesn't dip into my thoughts often, but picking up the bits I broadcast loud and clear is unavoidable. She's one of a handful of people who knows about my ability. And she was right, the Halloween regalia reminded me of, as she called it, home. Merope had been my residence for more than half my life, but a large piece of me couldn't forget my American upbringing.

"I'm being haunted," I said.

"By the people from the yacht?"

I nodded and spooned another glob of cake into my mouth. The confection was an explosion of sugar and bliss.

"And you want them to leave?"

Swallow. "They're annoying. Really annoying. There's a bunch of them and they're rude."

"Ghosts," she said, "I understand they can be bigger pests than rats if you let them. I was afraid this would happen sooner or later. Word is getting around the Afterlife that you're a person with certain skills."

She meant seeing the dead and my ability to find things. The first was congenital; the second was mostly persistence, with a dash of talent.

"But I've been able to see them forever, so why now?"

"It was probably your friend, Olga Marouli. Maybe she thought you could do some good, helping those who can no longer help themselves in the mortal world. Of course she should have asked your permission first, but I'm sure her intentions were the very best."

"How do I get rid of them? I asked nicely, then I asked rudely, then I made threats."

"And they refused?"

"They told me some ridiculous story about how they couldn't. According to them, they don't know how to *poof!* Allegedly."

"I imagine it's like any kind of leaving. You have to want to go."

"So I need to make the ghosts want to go?"

"Exactly. Entice them away or make your home inhospitable."

I chewed on the edge of my lip, rifling through my thin encyclopedia of ghost knowledge. What I knew was that I could see them. There was no entry shedding light on things ghosts hate. Exorcisms and sage were unknowns. They were movie tricks and the bailiwick of woo-woo people.

Weren't they?

Betty left her chair to go poking through the myriad ornate jars on the shop's shelves. She came back with a smudge stick.

"Sage works?"

"Sage works, although not always," she said. "Take it. Burn it. Open your front door and sweep toward that door. Shoo those spooks away. You have done everything you can for them. You tried to be helpful, and gave them good information, too. Not just any person would tell them about the Council for the Formerly Living. That's downright generous."

"Am I telegraphing my thoughts again?"

Her smile was warm and kind. It was a grandmotherly smile. "When you come in here you always relax, then it's like you're scribbling all your thoughts on billboards."

"What am I thinking right now?"

"You're wondering if I know all about that date you had with your handsome policeman."

Oof. Not good.

———

"Begone!" I waved the smoking sage around. "Scram! Vamoose! *Fyge*! Bugger off!" Being multilingual about ejecting these ghosts couldn't hurt.

Harry Vasiliakos and his posse watched me as I marched from room to room, smudging the whole apartment. When I was done, I grabbed my broom.

"Last chance to just get up and leave of your own accord," I warned them.

No takers. Great. Then it was time for them to feel my wrath—or what little wrath I had left late at night when I really wanted to be in bed. I yanked the front door open and began dragging the broom across the marble tile floor, out into the hallway.

Did the ghosts get up and *fyge?*

No, they did not.

What was it going to take?"

"Wow, you're really committed to housework," Lydia said. I whipped around to see my neighbor sashaying my way. Lydia is all hips, boobs, and hair that may or may not be naturally blonde. She's in her early twenties, and she makes most bad girls look like angels. Whether I liked her or not was undecided. I didn't *not* like her, but it's hard to get to know someone when neither of you is in a getting-to-know-anyone frame of mind. She'd lost her grandmother, almost lost her birth mother, and I'd lost my best friend. We were both dealing with that by keeping to ourselves. Lydia was just keeping to herself wearing fragments of black clothing (like me, she was in mourning) and rubbing against men in clubs because sometimes words don't always mean the same things to other people. I knew this because nothing travels faster than gossip. Light looks lazy and slow in comparison to the speed at which talk zips around Greece.

"Procrastination," I said. "It's sweep or work."

"Jimmy said to tell you that he told Leo you left a list for him."

"You were up at Leo's place?"

"No." She made a face. "Jimmy was outside. I think he has been hiding in the bushes."

"Like a dog."

"Like a dog," she agreed. "Is he normally like that?"

I held up a finger to my lips, then pointed to the stairs.

"I don't think anything about Jimmy is normal," I said in a louder than normal voice, "and I'm not talking about him being a *nanos*." *Nanos* is the Greek word for midget. It's impolite, but then so was Jimmy.

There was scuffling on the stairs, then Jimmy appeared, all one hundred and twenty centimeters of him. The Ugg boots were still on his feet but he'd lost the guy-liner.

"I heard that," he said.

"Maybe you shouldn't eavesdrop then."

"Can't a man walk up his own stairs without ridicule?"

I squinted at him. "Do you even live here?" I looked at Lydia, who would know, seeing as how she was technically Leo and Jimmy's landlord now. "Does he live here?"

She held up both hands. "Keep me out of this." And on that note she vanished into her apartment, leaving me with Jimmy and my broom. A moment later the German pop music started up again.

"Now look what you've done," Jimmy said, shaking his hands at the ceiling.

Why that little ... "Me? You're the eavesdropper. How is this my fault?"

He looked left, looked right, then dropped his voice to a whisper. "You know I like her."

"So do something about it."

What I could see of his face fell. "I can't."

"Sure you can. You're Jimmy Kontos. You're famous ... in some sticky circles."

"You're right." Gaining confidence, he nodded. "I'm kind of a big deal."

"I wouldn't say *big*."

I grabbed my broom, darted into my apartment, slammed the door. Jimmy's Ugg boots shuffled up to the narrow gap underneath. There was a small scuffling, then his voice wafted into the room."

"I can see your feet."

"Are you lying on the floor or are you really that short?"

"You stink," he whispered under the door. I guess he didn't want Lydia to hear what a little sawn-off *malakas* he could be.

When I turned around, the whole Vasilikos team was standing there. The women were all various shades of bored. *Kyrios* Harry was wearing a frown. He struck me as a man who wore one often and well.

"Why are you still here?"

"And miss the show?" *Kyrios* Harry said. "Your life is a disaster."

"It's not a disaster. The worst part of my life right now is standing in my apartment with his whole family."

One of his daughters giggled. She looked around at the rest of her bikini gang and the woman I assumed was her mother. "She thinks we're his family."

"You're not?"

"We're his companions," she said.

"You mean mistresses?"

A storm cloud wafted past her face. "Companions. We keep him company."

"And you're okay with this?" I asked the older woman with the stretched and tucked face.

"Why not? I am not his mother or his wife."

"I like young people," Harry said in his own defense, which, if you ask me, was no defense at all. Not one that would stand up in a court of human decency. "Not like that," he said, reading my mind.

"I don't care," I said.

"For that sort of thing I like older women," he said.

"I still don't care."

My phone rang. It was Betty.

"The sage and sweeping didn't work, did they?"

"How did you know?"

"Oh, your thoughts are like fireworks in the sky on the darkest night of the year, luv. Would you like me to send my brother over? He's familiar with a blessing or two that might fix your wee ghostie problem."

I looked at the ghosts infesting my apartment. "You guys are in for it now."

Harry's frown turned upside down in an approximation of what I thought was supposed to be a smile. It was toothy and sharklike and I didn't trust it one bit. "I am a businessman, Allie—can I call you Allie?—so let us make a deal."

"No deal. Just go."

"Solve my murder and I will tell you something you want to know," he said.

"People on Merope already tell me everything I want to know. For everything else, there's the internet. It can even tell me if the internet is supposed to have a capital letter. True story: it used to have a capital letter, but now it's perfectly acceptable to use a lowercase letter."

"There are some things the internet and gossiping peasants cannot tell you."

My one hand that wasn't holding the phone to my ear sat on my hip in the indignant position. "Like what?"

"I can tell you what happened to Andreas. I know where he is."

Shock rippled through me.

"Thank you," I told Betty, "but my life's plot just twisted."

"You know where to find me if you change your mind."

I ended the call and carefully set my phone on the table next to the front door. Then I looked at the King of Greek Bread, my heart breaking all over again in my chest.

"Tell me what you know about Andreas."

CHAPTER FOUR

HARRY VASILIKOS WAGGED his finger at me. "Quid pro quo. You help me, I help you."

"I already told you: I'm not a cop."

"But you are a detective of sorts, which means you can do things the police cannot, yes?

"Right but also wrong."

He didn't look like he gave a damn. "Think about it this way: the sooner you do what I want, the sooner you will get your information and your peace. And while you do that, I will be here waiting."

One of his—*cough, cough*—companions raised her hand. A dozen bangles slid down her arm, jangling like a bagful of empty soda cans. "Tell her to turn on the television. We are missing our shows."

Harry Vasilikos shrugged. "What my friends want, my friends want."

"This is my place. I do things my way."

"*Vre*, turn on the television for them," he said. "What can it hurt?"

My eye twitched. I found the remote. The television came to life. I flicked through the channels until the women clapped their hands and squealed. *Greece's Top Hoplite*. Figures.

"I just love Effie," one of the women said, hand on chest. It was a tiny hand on a lot of chest. Some of it was probably even real. She went to sit on the couch and fell through. The others laughed. They tried sitting. Same end result.

"Practice," I said. "You can do it."

This was ridiculous. Ghosts were basically holding my apartment and life hostage. But Harry Vasilikos had poked me right in the curiosity. I was burning to know what happened to Andreas, and had been since he left me on that blustery autumn evening.

My body had other plans. I yawned. My eyes filled with tears. Sleep wasn't optional, it was necessary.

"Where are you going?" the bread man wanted to know.

"Bed. If you have any complaints, tell someone who cares. That's not me, by the way. I'm your detective, not your therapist."

"So you will help me?"

"I don't have a choice."

———

Sometime during the night I woke up to the sound of footsteps on the floor above me. Leo Samaras was home. The ceiling creaked as he flopped down on his bed. All modern-era Greek homes are built earthquake-proof, with concrete and rebar skeletons, but sounds still travels, especially when you're a lot of man like Leo Samaras.

I lay there wondering how his night had gone, if he had any suspects in the Vasilikos murders, and whether or not any of those suspects were on the list I'd left for him. Did he know they were murders, or he had mistaken them for victims of a tragic accident?

Was he thinking about me?

I definitely wasn't thinking about him.

Eyes closed, I focused on other things. Sheep jumping over fences. That one embarrassing thing I did that time. Witty comebacks that would have been so much more helpful years ago. I replayed old arguments in my head, emerging as the more eloquent victor. In the middle of the night, and in my imagination, my verbal prowess was unparalleled.

More creaking. Footsteps. This time leading away from the bedroom.

Probably he went to get a glass of water.

I rolled over. Dead Cat snored. I solved Greece's economy problems and negotiated world peace. My thoughts jumped sideways to the ghost who used to sunbathe naked in our street back in the USA and how I'd winced every time someone drove through her. One time I asked her to move and she called me a party pooper. My mind leaped forward this time, to my date with Leo and its morbid ending.

Some jerk knocked on my door. And kept knocking.

Rude.

Cool air groped me as I sat up, so I took the warm covers with me, wrapping them around my shoulders. Dead Cat yowled.

"You're dead." I shoved my feet into fuzzy slippers. "You don't even need blankets."

The knocking continued. Someone really had their *sovraka* bunched up, right in the crack.

That someone was Detective Leo Samaras. He was in sweats and a ball cap, and somehow he managed to look like he was on his way to a photoshoot. That couldn't be natural. Bags under his eyes were my saving grace. They were carrying purple-grey luggage, and that luggage was carrying luggage. Hideous. He was practically a monster.

"Do you know what time it is?" I didn't and I was hoping he could tell me.

He held out a familiar piece of paper. "What is this?"

I eyed the sheet of paper I'd left for him. "It's called paper. We used to use it in the days before we started doing everything on computers and phones."

His full lips quirked. "I mean the names on the paper."

"Oh. Suspects in the Vasilikos murders."

His forehead scrunched up. "Vasilikos murders?"

Harnessing the power of shadow puppets, I made one of my hands crash into the other hand repeatedly on the living room wall. "Boat go *BOOM*."

"The yacht?"

"You're sexy *and* smart."

A delicious grin spread across his face. "You think I'm sexy?"

"I think I'm tired." I went to close the door. "I need sleep."

He stopped the door with his hand. "What murder suspects? It was an accident. The yacht collided with the island and the whole thing went up in flames. And anyway, how did you come up with a list of" he looked at the paper "suspects?"

I yawned. Pulled the covers tighter around me. "Research. I did some serious investigating, called in some favors, and found out who might have wanted Harry Vasilikos dead."

"Wait—that's Harry Vasilikos's yacht? Harry Vasilikos the millionaire?"

"Well, it was. Now it's not anybody's anything."

He shook his head like he was clearing cobwebs. "I'm lost. How do you know it was his yacht?"

"The Royal Pain? Thirty seconds of Googling. You didn't Google it?"

"No." His shoulders slumped. The man was exhausted. I wanted to reel him inside, fix him a hot meal. Too bad our one date had turned into hell and now I didn't want to be stuck in a non-public place with him. "We've been busy hauling bodies out of the water. Gus has got the bodies now. It's not a homicide so there's no need for me to pull an all-nighter."

"So you're saying nobody on the boat was dead before the accident?"

"Why would they be?"

"Just a hunch, but maybe someone—someone on that list —killed them before the crash. And maybe that same someone sabotaged the yacht to cover up their crime."

He tipped back his head and laughed. "This isn't a laughing matter, but you're funny. Where did you get these ideas?"

"I pull them out of my *kolos* for fun. You should hear my theories about the first moon landing."

He leaned against the doorframe and fixed those baggy, bruised eyes on me. "What's your theory about the first moon landing?"

"That Americans were really there and Neil Armstrong was really the first man to walk on the moon."

Harry Vasilikos was hovering nearby, listening. From the scowl on his face I'd say he was either annoyed or—

"Who is this *malakas*?" he asked, pompous and puffed up.

Annoyed. Definitely annoyed.

I couldn't respond. Leo didn't know the dead were as real to me as the living—and why would he? It was my dirty little secret. Always had been.

Without making eye contact with Kyrios Harry, I went

on. "At least consider the possibility that they were murdered beforehand. And if I'm right, look at the names on this list, okay?"

Leo blew out a long, frustrated sigh. "Okay."

"Go get some sleep," I told him.

"You want to come with me?" He went to grin but it fell right off when he saw my expression shift from sleepy to horrified. "Sorry."

"It's okay," I said, even though it was nothing like okay. "You should go."

He pushed a hand though his dark hair and nodded. "We should talk. Not tonight, but soon."

"I don't think so," I said. Slowly, I closed the door. Blankets tight around my shoulders, back flat against the door, I sighed.

"Disaster," Kyrios Harry said.

"I'm going back to bed. If you follow me, my next phone call will be to an exorcist."

———

Morning body-slammed me.

No. Wait. That was Dead Cat, who had a lot of weight for something that wasn't technically there. His favorite game was where he jumped onto my dresser and took a flying leap onto me ... while I was sleeping. My terrified shrieks brought him joy.

Slowly, I eased the purring lump off me and swung my legs out of bed. I yawned, stretched, made myself all kind of promises about how I would eat healthy today, how I would always take off my makeup before bed from now on, and that I would do my Christmas shopping in January, starting from next year. Then I nixed the idea because I had a niece and nephew who collected and discarded five new interests every morning before breakfast.

My intentions were good. That's what mattered.

I stood, yawned some more, brushed the hair out of my eyes.

Then I screamed.

CHAPTER FIVE

"Two rooms are off limits," I said, ticking them off on my fingers. "The bathroom and my bedroom. You don't sleep and you don't have bodily functions or hygiene needs, therefore you have no business in either room. Nod if you all understand."

Harry Vasilikos and his crew of plastic princesses nodded. We were in my bedroom, where I'd caught them all practicing walking through walls.

"Now you need to go hang out in the living room or kitchen, because I need to shower and get dressed.

"Why bother?" one of the women I'd mistaken for Harry's daughter said. "It's not like you have any good clothes anyway."

"I have good clothes—great clothes. They're perfect for my job, which is blending in with my surroundings. Also, get out of my bedroom now."

She shrugged, one "whatever" away from being an American teenager.

Half an hour later, I straggled back into the living room, where the ghosts were huddled around the television again.

Apparently this channel was a slow-drip diet of trash TV, so they were entertained, for now. They almost had the hang of sitting on real furniture; only their butts were in the couch now.

I grabbed my bag, my phone, and my keys, and bolted before Kyrios Harry decided he wanted to have another conversation.

It was time to plot out my day. So far, the only thing on my list was leaving my apartment, and I'd already accomplished that. Which meant the day was looking good. I jogged across the street for some self-flagellation at Merope's Best.

Merope's Best makes Merope's worst—coffee, that is. Their beans are singed, and sometimes the coffee comes with suspicious hairs. They sell fancy coffees rather than the traditional Greek fare. That means half the island flocks here so they can say they're sipping a latte with a shot of who-knows-what—possibly goat saliva or chickpeas.

I scooted past a table of dead teenagers (they'd lost a game of chicken on the mainland; speeding Smart Forfour never beats the flank of a manure truck) and ordered something Italian-sounding with a bunch of caramel and plenty of caffeine.

"You must hate yourself," the barista said. His teeth were chattering. His eyeballs were red. His T-shirt read "Coffee or Die" in several languages.

"Only after I drink your coffee."

"I know what you mean."

I grabbed my coffee and took it outside, just in case my stomach rejected the drink. Soon the caffeine would kick in and I'd be able to think. For something dreadful it wasn't so bad, like a trip to the gynecologist. And three sips in— *whoosh!*—just like that, the clouds parted. My eye twitched, and my heart began to complain about how I should really see a cardiologist if I was going to abuse it this way every morning and sometimes in the afternoon.

I sat on the curb, poking a small stone with my boot. I couldn't say I was enjoying the coffee but the clarity it gave me was helpful.

What first?

Getting rid of the ghosts was my top priority. To get rid of the ghosts I had to solve their murders. Despite his muttered promises that he'd look into it, I knew Leo wouldn't treat this like a homicide unless the evidence pointed in that direction. And that evidence was lying in Merope's morgue, burned to a crisp. Which meant I would have to go poking around on my own, hunting for the equivalent of fingerprints on a murder weapon.

Solve the crime and get rid of the ghosts.

And then find out what Harry Vasilikos knew about Andreas.

———

My recycled paper cup was almost empty and I hadn't thrown up yet. Definitely a good omen. So what did I have, besides a cast iron stomach?

A list of suspects, none of whom lived here.

I dumped what was left of my coffee in the garbage can outside Merope's Best and jogged back upstairs to my apartment. All was quiet across the hall. No kicky German pop. Since Lydia moved in it was like Eurovision around here.

Inside, the ghost women were still watching television, even the dour woman I'd mistaken for Kyria Vasilikos.

"Where is your wife?" I asked Harry Vasilikos, who was standing at the window, watching the sea. "She wasn't on the yacht, was she?"

"Nowhere, that's where she is. Have you solved my case yet?"

Angela had mentioned the bread baron never married. That small detail had slipped my memory. It came back to me now.

"I have questions."

"Questions are good. They show you are curious and invested." He turned around. "Ask your questions."

I flipped my laptop's lid and opened a new file. "Where were you sailing from before the yacht crashed?"

"The Sporades."

"Business or pleasure?"

"Yes."

Oh boy. Different angle: "Why were you in the Sporades?"

"Business meetings with potential distributers."

"Bringing Royal Pain bread to the islands?"

"Yes. I do not like untapped markets. It means I am lazy, and I am not a lazy man."

"What was the outcome of the meeting?"

"Not positive. But give me time." His eyes closed. He let out a string of colorful, anatomically impossible curses involving Jesus Christ's *mouni,* a monkey, and a horn. For his generation he was sure being progressive; good for him for considering the possibility that Jesus was a woman. "Time is one thing I do not have."

"For what I understand, you have an infinite amount of time but no body to spend it in."

He stared at me. Hard. "That was very helpful."

"Helpful Allie, that's me. So the Sporades islands said 'Oxi' to Royal Pain bread?"

Oxi is the Greek word for "no." It's also famously the one word the Greek prime minister said to Mussolini when Il Duce demanded access to Greece or face war. Greece said, "No," and chose war. I wasn't convinced; Greek's aren't normally restrained enough to limit their refusals to a single word when that much is at stake. Toula always gave me a dirty look when I mentioned that the prime minister, being completely Greek, must have thrown at least one "*malaka*" in there.

"For now," Kyrios Harry said.

That sounded vaguely ominous. Maybe Harry Vasilikos was a man who easily cultivated enemies in business. Any of one them might enjoy watching him sink to the bottom of the Aegean Sea. Any of them might have wanted to give him a helping hand or foot, say on the top of his head.

I jotted down his answers, adding my own thoughts. "Your trip to Merope, was that business, too?"

"Of course. Why else would I come here?"

Inside my head, I raised a sarcastic and judgmental eyebrow. "The beaches, the women, the food. The same reason anyone comes here."

"The beaches and food I can get on any Greek island. The women ... Women are everywhere."

"*Oink.*"

"What did you say?"

"Nothing," I said. "I sneezed. Who was your business meeting supposed to be with here?"

"Yiorgos and Dimitri Triantafillos. Do you know them?"

"They own the Super Super Market and the More Super Market. Did they express an interest in stocking Royal Pain bread?"

"No. I came here to convince them."

"Convince them how?"

"Wine, women, and money."

My gaze slid to the women-children gathered in my living room. "Those women?"

"Not these women. They are just girls."

There are dinosaur bones younger than Yiorgos and

Dimitri Triantafillos. No way would they respond to Kyrios Harry's companions—or any other woman—without pharmaceutical intervention and a cardiac unit on standby.

"Have you ever actually met the Triantafillou brothers before?"

"Why?"

"Unless the woman was shaped like a pile of money, I doubt they'd be interested. Just a few more questions. You were all killed before you crashed into Merope, yes?"

"Correct."

"Was it before you left the Sporades or while you were en route to Merope?"

"Somewhere between the Sporades and this place. We were on the open water."

I wrote down his answer. "Was there anyone else on the boat?"

"No."

"Who was piloting the boat?"

He shrugged. "I always pilot my own yacht. Since I was a small boy, I have owned a boat. Not a yacht at first because there was a time when my family had nothing, but I always had a boat, even if it was made of leaking planks."

"How were you killed?"

"Poison."

"Poison? That's potentially inefficient, although I suppose the alleged killer succeeded. What was poisoned?"

"The water, the food, I don't know. We were all eating, drinking, and then we were vomiting and dying."

If I could get to the yacht, maybe there'd be enough of it left for me to go hunting for clues, and by clues I meant leftover food and drink.

Click. Save.

I was out of here.

The scene of the accident was devoid of life signs this morning. Either everyone was in their beds or they'd stripped every bit of information from the yacht's bones and were busy elsewhere in analysis mode.

I stood on the cliff and looked down at the wreckage, pondering my next probably-illegal move.

"You could always fall," the ghost woman with the 90's hairstyle said. "I did."

"Yes, and look how that turned out."

"Where is your compassion?" she said, leaping to her doom again.

I waited until she popped back in to position. "You're the one who keeps falling."

"I can't help myself."

What had Betty told me? Ghosts have to want to go. Whether they're popping back to the Afterlife or *poofing* around town, they have to want it. The woman brightened up when I passed on the happy news.

"Really?"

She closed her eyes, crossed herself, forehead to chest, shoulder to shoulder, then she tumbled over the edge, same as always.

One ... two ... three ...

Poof! She didn't look happy or impressed. "It didn't work."

"I guess you didn't want it hard enough."

Big sigh. "I hate falling more than ever now. It's a mess down there. All kinds of garbage floating in the water. I could get a disease. Very unhygienic."

"Relax. Death brings all your vaccinations up to date." Her other words sank in. "Garbage? What kind of garbage?" Without my binoculars, the yacht was a lump of fiberglass and other materials. If there was garbage it was hidden by the foamy churn.

"Why do you care about garbage?"

"Clues. Evidence."

The yacht's remains were unreachable without a boat. I didn't have a boat. So I called my parents' other daughter.

"Do you own a boat?" I asked Toula.

"Why would we own a boat?"

"For maritime activities?"

"We don't have a boat."

"How about a jetpack?"

Toula sighed like I was her third child; which, for the record, I wasn't. "What are you doing, Allie?"

My boot-covered toe nudged the stone, pushed it along the curb. "Talking to you on the phone, what else? Have you heard from our parents?"

"When I hear from them, I'll let you know."

Wow, what was her problem? Her tone was tighter than a bouzouki string.

"Something wrong?"

"Milos and Patra are home today." The words rode out on a sigh.

"But it's a weekday. Why aren't they in school?" Dumb question. Toula and I spoke at the same time. "Strike."

Greek teachers strike a lot. They always want something, and that something is always money. Greece's coffers are filled with IOUs, empty promises, and the scent of money; and apparently teachers (and other government employees) can't buy life's necessities using any of those things.

"Want me to take them for a while?"

"No, it's fine. I'm fine." She lowered the phone and let out the long, primal howl of a wounded beast. When she recovered she said, "LEGO. I just stood on LEGO."

Wince. "I'll let you go so you can get that foot amputated now."

"It's the only way," she said.

So what did I have now besides a list of absent suspects? No boat, obviously. A jetpack was out of the question. Renting a boat was a possibility, although difficult outside of tourist season. Rappelling was a less viable option, but I liked the idea of hovering midair over the wreck. It had a *Mission Impossible* flavor to it.

A boat it would have to be.

Thirty minutes later, I was the proud temporary owner of a floating tin can the size of a bathtub. Its motor was a pair of immersion blenders, strapped together with duct tape. Good thing it came with a couple of oars, too. Did I say oars? My mistake. I meant *koutalas*—wooden spoons. Five minutes after the rental place took custody of my money and I took custody of the approximation of a real boat (the better boats —the actual boats—were moored for the winter), I was puttering around the island's outer curve, bound for the crash site. On this chilly morning I was alone on the water, which was more gray than summer's blue-green. It was the color of skulking krakens and Poseidon's imminent Seasonal Affective Disorder. I tried not to think about what was lurking below as the immersion blenders coughed and gagged. I helped them along by rowing. In the distance, far away from Merope's rocks, fishermen were hoisting nets out of the sea, dumping them on deck, dipping them into the water again. Without an onslaught of tourists to hoover up their daily catches, they were moving slowly.

There she was, the Royal Pain. The vessel looked bigger from down here, even though it was crushed like a soda can. Merope had packed one heck of a punch. The yacht never stood a chance, not at the speed it was moving.

Who had set that speed, and where did they go? Harry

Vasilikos and his guests couldn't have poisoned themselves and then set the speed to *annihilate*. But Harry Vasilikos was his own captain, so that's probably exactly what he did, inadvertently. Set the autopilot, destination: Merope. Then he went off to eat his bowl of poison.

The tin can drifted around the wreckage, which was no longer burning. The sea air had whisked away most of the smoke and its acrid smell. Garbage bobbed around the yacht's white, bloated corpse. Some was floating out to sea, bound for (eventually) Greece's other islands. Most of the refuse was bumping against the rock, pushed and pulled by the tide. Clothing, gadgets, bits of the boat itself. A soggy pillow was beached on one of the island's vicious crags. A rubbery dildo had fastened its suction cap to a smooth expanse of rock and was flopping up and down in the breeze.

If Leo and I were a thing, I'd snap a picture and send it to him. Then we would laugh and make jokes before one us suggested it would be a fun purchase, you know, just for kicks. Then either an uncomfortable silence would set in or the whole thing would be foreplay. But we weren't, so I didn't.

I nudged the boat-ish thing closer, hoping to find anything that might still have traces of the poison Harry Vasilikos mentioned. A couple of water bottles were drifting near the hull, so I scooped them into a plastic bag, along with some pieces of fruit. Other food—bread, cheese—had disintegrated or drowned in Merope's waters.

As far as evidence went, that was the only thing that stood out. For more, I would have to board what was left of the yacht. Trying it alone didn't seem smart, but trying it with others might earn me a slap on the wrist and one of Leo's frowny faces. The way things were between us, I didn't want to be on the receiving end of his frowny face. I didn't want to see his face at all.

Lying to myself was working out really well. Definitely one of my hidden talents.

Then my phone rang. Whoever was calling, they weren't in my contacts.

"What are you doing?" a male voice wanted to know.

"Who is this?"

"Look up."

Constable Gus Pappas was peering over the cliff's edge. He had coffee in one hand and he was using the other as a visor, despite the fact that he was wearing dark aviators.

"Nothing to see here," I said into the phone. "I'm not the woman you're looking for."

"Ha-ha. A *Star Wars* joke. I like it. Seriously, what are you doing?"

"What does it look like I'm doing?"

He took a short pull from his cup and made a face. Someone had stopped at Merope's Best.

"I'm not an expert, but I would say you are looking for loot."

"Wrong. I'm looking for clues."

"Clues? What kind of clues?"

"*Blue's Clues.*"

"I don't know what that is, but you should probably finish what you're doing and leave. Everyone else will be back soon."

"Why? They're not finished the rescue operation?"

He opened his mouth but Call Waiting chose that moment to cut in. This time the number was one I knew.

"You were right," Leo said, his voice grim. "They were dead before the yacht crashed."

CHAPTER SIX

I WAS on dry land again, my sardine can returned to its owner. Getting my security deposit back had been a battle, right up until I threatened to park my bicycle in front of the boat rental place all summer, while I scared potential customers away with true customer service horror stories. The owner knew me, and I knew that one time—at least—he'd tried to engage in oral sex with a donkey. He wound up in the hospital with a hoof print on his cheek and some convenient memory loss. But there was a witness (wasn't there always?), and that witness had parted with the juicy story while we were reaching for the same watermelon five summers ago. I could barely look at the man without hearing Wayne Newton singing *Donkey Shame*.

As I was escaping with my deposit in hand, Leo was pulling up at the dock. If he'd slept at all it didn't show. He was wearing the same combination of jeans, boots, black sweater, and leather jacket he'd been wearing yesterday. The circles under his eyes were dinner plates.

"Say it again," I said.

"Which part?"

"The part where I'm right."

He chuckled. "You were right. Now I need to know how you knew."

I jumped in with a question of my own before answering. "Did Panos start the autopsies?"

Panos Grekos is Merope's coroner. He's abrupt, moody, and he gets all his pornography the old school way: from a *periptero*—a newsstand. His dead mother haunts his favorite *periptero*, shrieking like a banshee when Panos shows up for the latest Playboy. She doesn't know I can see and hear her, or I have no doubt she would destroy my sanity until I agreed to convert her son into a Good Greek Boy.

"He started when the first body showed up. According to him, every body we recovered had been dead for at least three hours before the crash."

"Any idea how they died?"

"None. We know what it wasn't, and that's all we know." He fixed those long-lashed eyes of his on me. "You didn't answer my question."

Focus on the bags, Allie. "You didn't ask one."

"How did you know they were dead prior to the crash?"

I shrugged. "A ghost told me."

A smile crept into his eyes. "A ghost? Let me guess. Harry Vasilikos's ghost?"

"Of course."

He laughed, full and deep. "Ghosts. The way you say it I almost believe you."

"Almost?"

The laugh went away. "You're a smart woman. You don't strike me as ..." he wiggled his fingers.

"Woo-woo?"

"Like one of those old Greek women who sees signs and spirits everywhere. You don't spit when you say something nice about someone. I'm a policeman and I believe in hard evidence. Supernatural, paranormal, whatever you want to call it, I don't believe in it because it's not there, it doesn't exist."

"And people who do believe in those things?"

"Crazy."

My heart crashed down through my lungs and diaphragm, leaving me winded. Leo and I had no future—or a past—but it stung that his opinion of people like me was so low. I'd made the right call, exiting the restaurant stage left. Well, not stage left. I'd wriggled out the bathroom window like I was leaving the scene of a horrendous toilet crime.

"I have to go," I said, and it wasn't a lie. The junk I'd fished out of the water needed analyzing, so I had somewhere else to be as soon as possible.

Leo nodded, his brain somewhere else. "I have to get moving, too. I hope we recovered all the passengers yesterday."

"How many did you get?"

"Six. Why?"

Mentally, I counted my apartment's occupants, then I counted them again. Both times I came up with one extra. Seven. A small bell rang in my head. Betty had also mentioned the number six. At the time, I figured all the bodies hadn't been recovered yet.

"You're missing one," I said. "There should be seven."

"Your ghost again?"

I held up both hands, wiggled my fingers. "I have powers you can't imagine, and I used to them to get a headcount."

———

Sam Washington lives outside the village, halfway up the hill. Which is a real pain in his black ass, as he puts it. If he'd had access to a physic, he swears he would have bought a place on one of Merope's flatter surfaces because dragging that wheelchair up the hill is living out its welcome. If Sam sounds like an American, that's because he is. Sam came to Merope hunting for a missing person. He quickly discovered two things when he arrived: his missing person wasn't missing. The guy had followed his *poutsa* across several Greek islands, narrowly avoiding fathers with shovels, pitchforks, and other assorted garden tools. The second thing Sam discovered was that he and Merope were soulmates. Business was good, there was money to be made, and he could do it here in a low-stress environment, where a traffic jam was two bicycles and one old man on a donkey. From Merope he could go anywhere in Europe, if the work paid.

On my last day of high school I begged Sam for a job. He liked that we spoke the same language—literally—so he hired me to be his overworked, underpaid sidekick. When I established Finders Keepers, Sam was my first client. Hit and run. Turned out a seven-year-old had struck him with a car and kept on going. End result: cool, shiny wheelchair for Sam, and a lifetime supply of figs from the boy's family.

"The dudes always dig a man with his own wheels," Sam always says. "If that doesn't seal the deal, the figs win them over."

"What do you think?" I said to Sam today. I was holding up two bags. One held garbage. The second was packed full of treats from the Cake Emporium. The white cakebox was waiting when I walked into what had become my favorite store on Merope.

("I know what Sam likes," Betty had said. "Call it a very well-educated guess. The bodies on these bats are filled with tiramisu.")

"Only one of those bags is full of good eats, and it's not the one with ..." Sam squinted "... is that trash? Did you bring this fine looking black man a bag of garbage?"

"It's your lucky day. The cakes are for you. The trash is for some other poor person who can check it for traces of poison."

"Who?"

"I was hoping you could give me a name."

When it comes to knowing stuff, Sam Washington knows more than me. He has been collecting names and people since Aretha Franklin was skinny—his words, not mine. These days he is more of a tech guy, although he dabbles in private investigating, when the lucre is less filthy and more lucrative. After the hit-and-run, he took every online computer class available and discovered he had a knack of hacking the unhackable.

"Nobody on Merope. Plenty of people you can buy poison from, but no one who analyzes the stuff. Even the cops outsource to a lab on the mainland. How quick do you need an answer?"

"There's no ticking clock, but soon would be great."

He held out his hand. "Give me your trash, woman, then give me that cake."

I grabbed a fork and unpacked the cakebox.

Sam raised an eyebrow. He was good at it. "One fork? You sick or something? Let me guess: you didn't make up with that cute cop yet."

"There's no making up to do."

"Uh-huh."

"It was one date. It didn't work out."

"Half a date."

I lifted out a tiramisu bat, placed it on the plate, passed it to Sam, whose eyes widened to saucers.

"What's this? Greeks eat some funny things but I didn't know they ate bats."

"Just shut up and eat it, Ozzie," I said, laughing.

He shrugged and stuck the fork in. One bite later he was

swooning. "I don't know where you got this, Callas, but I'm telling you whoever baked this is a magician." When I told him about the Cake Emporium, he shook his head and swallowed another bite. "Never heard of it, but this might be worth rolling down the hill for. So you gonna tell me what makes a woman cut out of a date and shimmy out the bathroom window?"

"I realized he was a bad idea."

"Yeah, I've had a few of those myself." He didn't seem too broken up about it, but that was Sam for you.

"Anyone new on the horizon?"

"Please, you keep me too busy with your trash." His voice was gruff but his eyes were all sparkle.

"Keep it up, Washington, and I'll put the rest of those cakes on the high shelf."

"You are one cruel woman."

He ate. Not hungry, for once, I watched him enjoy the cakes Betty's brother had whipped up. We took turns mocking each other and faking outrage, until my phone heralded the arrival of a new text message. I ignored it. Reality was trying to cut into my fun time.

"You want to tell me what happened on that date?"

"No."

"Tell me anyway."

Sam knew my little secret. He didn't judge, didn't think I was weird. He did see how dead people could potentially be a real pain in the behind. Now that Olga was gone, Sam was the closest thing I had to a best friend. Maybe my only real friend. Lots of people talk to me but it tends to be a one-way transaction. My life is acquaintance-rich.

So I told Sam about how Leo and I decided on Taverna! Taverna! Taverna! for our date night. Nice place. Dumb name. No prizes for guessing the owner's favorite WWII movie. Though the night was cool, Taverna! Taverna! Taverna! had exterior gas heating, for those rare tourists and less rare locals who wanted to dine alfresco during the colder months. We both wore jeans but I went all out with a fancy top and a good jacket. My lipstick was red and my eye makeup was smoky. Somewhere along the way I'd managed to figure out how to draw the perfect winged eye without jabbing my eyeball with the liquid liner. Leo told me I looked pretty, and the way he checked me out—hard and all over—told me he meant it.

The first ghost showed up while we were picking at *mezedes* and I was forking a chunk of spanakopita into my mouth. She was young, beautiful, and as dead as dead gets. She held up her wrists and bled invisible-to-regular-people blood prettily onto the food. I nudged the plate away and tried to ignore the dramatic visual retelling of her death.

"This will be you," she said. "You will see."

My teeth sank into my tongue. What was Leo saying? Something about my sister, Toula. Perfect. Everyone wants to hear about their date's exes over dinner, especially when that ex is their sister.

I shook my head, tried to focus. "What about Toula?"

"She came to see me at work."

"Why?"

His forehead had scrunched up. He'd genuinely looked worried. "Are you okay?"

Nod. "Why did Toula come to see you at work?"

"She didn't say. It was strange. Is everything okay with her?"

Strange? He didn't know strange. "As far as I know."

Ghost Woman One was joined by Ghost Woman Two. Tall. Thin. The kind of beautiful normally created by Photoshop. Ghost Woman Two had a pair of pantyhose wrapped around her delicate, crooked neck. She choked for several long minutes, face purpling. Then she straightened up and perched her perky *kolos* on the table's blue-and-white edge while her friend bled.

"This is all pantyhose are good for." Ghost Woman Two smiled down at me with full, red Max Factor lips. "And all he is good for is killing women."

"A killer," the bleeder agreed. "He made this look like a suicide. Convincing, yes? He is very talented."

"Talented and deadly. You should run away now. Save yourself. If only we could have saved ourselves."

"But we never saw it coming." The first woman wiped her wrist on a passing waiter. To me, his shirt looked like a used maxi pad but the poor guy had no clue. "The beautiful murderer."

"He is beautiful," the choker agreed.

Killing women? Detective Leo Samaras? My skin goose-pimpled. Sour acid sloshed around in my previously starving stomach. I jerked in my seat. My elbow bumped my glass. Water everywhere.

Leo surged forward, napkin in hand. He mopped my dress but it was pointless—this mess, this dinner, was unfixable.

I got up. I left via the bathroom window. I didn't look back.

In the here and now, Sam's face was passive, curious. I knew that face; my former boss was in information gathering mode. "You think he killed those women?"

"I don't know."

"Want to know what I'd do?"

"I know what you'd do because it's the same thing I'd do." Check homicides, suicides, and missing persons until I found those faces.

"But you haven't done it yet, have you?"

"No."

"Let me ask you something."

I snorted. "Like I could stop you."

Sam laughed, loud and deep. "You know me too well. Okay, my question is this: Why do you think your sister went to see him?"

"The only reason I can think of is that she considers him her property and wants him to stay away from me."

"Why is that? She's married, got herself a couple of cute kids, a home, a business."

"Because he's her ex and it would be weird if we were together—for all of us. Or maybe because, on some level, she still wants to ride the Leo train."

"Or maybe she knows that boy ain't right. Maybe she can't articulate what exactly it is that's wrong with him, but her animal brain knows. You want me to do some digging for you?"

"You don't know what the dead women look like."

"Doesn't mean I can't poke around, see if he's got any skeletons in that closet of his."

"Not yet." I wanted to be the one with the shovel, but I wasn't there yet. Denial wasn't just a river in Egypt. The longer I delayed digging, the longer I'd be able to stay hopeful. I didn't want Leo to be a murderer.

He tapped his cheek. "Then give me some sugar and get going."

I kissed Sam's cheek and hugged the stuffing out him.

On the other side of Sam's front door, a surprise was waiting, a surprise I hoped would never darken my doorstep.

"Aliki Callas, I have not seen you in church recently." Kyria Sofia wagged her white-gloved finger at me. Kyria Sofia's brother Father Spiros is the priest at Ayios Konstantinos—Saint Constantine. This means Kyria Sofia has taken the heavy burden of being the island's morality police upon her slim shoulders—shoulders that were, today, encased in a navy blue skirt suit with her favorite ladybug brooch pinned to the lapel. The hand that wasn't wagging a finger at me was lightly gripping a wicker basket, filled with loaves of bread and wrapped parcels of cheese and deli meats.

"I've been thinking about going, and it's the thought that counts."

She smiled. Bright. Wide. Faker than Astroturf. "No, the thought does not count at all. Only actions count." She held the basket out to Sam. "I'm here to do Christ and the Virgin Mary's work. Helping cripples is the best part of my day."

Somehow I doubted that. The priest's sister possessed the largest collection of bestiality porn in the country. She kept it all on safely hidden on her computer in a folder labelled "Sewing". And just between us, her most-viewed file involved a "romantic" encounter between a man, a billygoat, and a jumbo-sized can of feta.

Sam accepted the basket. "This *cripple*" he pressed lightly on the word "thanks you."

Kyria Sofia tittered. "Your Greek is getting so good, I almost forget you are black."

My eye twitched.

"Aliki," she went on, not giving a fig about her casual racism, "a *poulaki* told me you were there when that yacht crashed."

A *poulaki* is a little bird. It's also slang for a small penis. If I were a betting woman, I would not put my money on the bird feeding her that story.

When I confirmed the rumor, she nodded. "Such a tragedy. I knew Harry Vasilikos, of course."

"From here on Merope?"

"Of course. He used to come often, but not for many years. I do not know why he stopped coming." She smiled. It was the smile of someone plotting social destruction. "Come to church soon, both of you, eh? Otherwise people will talk."

People would talk—they always did—but what Kyria Sofia

didn't mention was that all gossip and rumors would be started by her.

She waved goodbye and slithered back to the street on squat, sensible heels.

"That was nice of her," I said, deadpan.

Sam grimaced. "I'm the only black man that woman has ever met. She's dying to know if the rumors are true."

———

Like most days on Merope, this one was shaping up to have a lot of sun in it. Now there was enough heat in the rays for me to discard my top layer. I stuffed it into my bicycle's basket and considered my next move. Angela's man of the moment was still absent, so I scrolled through my email and voicemail and picked out the easiest, least time-consuming jobs. I grabbed a satisfying, non-toxic coffee at a *kafeneio* that wasn't Merope's Best and sat at one of the outdoor tables in a patch of gentle sun.

Almost immediately, I located a heating pad large enough for a donkey and placed the order for one of the local elderly men, who didn't have internet access or anything to access it with. His donkey was almost as old as he was, and in the colder months the animal's joints ached.

The male half of a recently married couple was convinced his bride was cheating, and he wanted me to find out who she was banging and why—and did he have a bigger *poutsa* than my client? The Merope grapevine had already solved this one. His wife wanted to make a little extra cash, so she'd taken on a job as a *sisa* cook, whipping up cheap Greek meth for other housewives. She couldn't brew the illegal drug at home, so while her husband was at work she was sneaking off to one of the island's abandoned houses to do her cooking.

I messaged him back and told him he had bigger problems than a cheating wife. Relieved that she wasn't cheating, and more than a little proud that she displayed ambition and an entrepreneurial spirit, he paid my fee in full, with a bonus.

Forrest Gump was wrong. Life wasn't like a box of chocolates; people were.

While I was sifting through small cases, my brain was gnawing on the Vasilikos murders. Kyria Sofia, using one of her two faces, had mentioned this wasn't Harry's first trip to Merope. If she remembered him, maybe others did too. I wasn't sure which local thread to pull first, so I checked out the list of suspects Harry had given me and crosschecked it with business owners in the Sporades. Not everyone, or every business, is connected to the internet in Greece, so I had to go swimming outside my regular information pool.

Jackpot on the first search. Penny Papadopoulo, the first name on the list, owned the largest, most profitable supermarket on the island of Skiathos in the Sporades. Sixty seconds later, Penny was on the other end of my phone, laughing. Her receptionist had patched me right through the moment I'd mentioned Kyrios Harry's name and death in the same sentence.

"Are you serious, Harry Vasilikos is dead?"

"His yacht crashed into Merope, but he was already dead by that point."

She laughed and laughed and laughed. When I thought she was done laughing, she laughed some more. "Good. Now I will not have to kill him myself."

"You didn't like him?"

"He was *skata*. Rich *skata*, but *skata*."

"What happened?" The American in me wanted to add a disclaimer such as "If you don't mind me asking", but this was Greece, so I did it the direct, Greek way.

"He expected me to *hezo* all over the local bakers by selling his bread. Have you tried it? It tastes like *archidia*."

Some balls tasted pretty good, and by the size of Harry's yacht I figured a lot of other people agreed.

"Our island doesn't sell his bread."

"Neither does ours, and it never will. The bakers would riot if we started selling his bread. They would go out of business. How could I sleep at night? I was born and raised on Skiathos. This is my home, and these are my people. I own a supermarket that has been in my family for decades. We all do what we can to maintain balance, so we can all survive, especially in this economy."

Her words made sense. Not everybody embraced the cutthroat business model of dominating the market, hoarding all the money, and sleeping on it like one of Tolkien's dragons.

"According to the police, everyone on the yacht was dead before the boat crashed."

"Dead how?"

"I don't know."

"Maybe someone did not like his bread."

I didn't tell her she was on the suspect list. Sooner or later Detective Samaras would be in touch; he could give her the bad news.

"What happened when you turned down his offer?"

"He offered me more money."

"And when you didn't accept that?"

"He left. But first he reminded me that he could burn down my business, and I reminded him that Royal Pain is not the only bakery in Greece—just the worst."

"Who was his main competition, do you know?"

"You are on Merope, you say? You might know the family. The owner was Thanassi Dalaras. The business is owned by his widow now, although according to the papers she does not play an active role in the company."

"What's his widow's name?"

"I don't remember. All I know is she lives on Merope, and Wundebar Bread is currently run by Yiannis Margas."

I froze.

The name rang a bell. A really big, grubby, tarnished bell. Margas's name was on the suspect list, but that's not all. With everything going on, my brain had missed the connection. Yiannis is the Greek form of John. John—Johnny Margas was Angela's new fling, the one she had me watching for.

I thanked Penny Papadopoulo for her time, then spent several minutes staring out to sea, wondering if one of the specks on the horizon was Johnny Margas's ride. Then I called Angela.

"How did you connect with Johnny?"

"Why? What is wrong?"

"Nothing. Yet."

"We met on a message board for rich people."

There was a whole world out there, and it was strange.

"Do you know what he does?"

"He is a businessman."

I banged my head on the table. The waiter came loping over, order pad in hand.

"One more?"

"One more," I told him. "Angela," I said into the phone, "was one of your husbands Thanassi Dalaras?"

"My first husband," she said.

"I don't suppose you own a bakery?"

"Maybe. I own lots of things."

Bang! went my head again.

"What are you doing?" Angela asked me.

"Banging my head on this table."

"Why?"

"Johnny Margas handles the day-to-day business operations of Wundebar Bread."

"That name sounds familiar."

"It used to belong to Thanassi Dalaras, your first husband— your first and dead husband—and given that he never sold it to anyone else, it's probably still yours and has been for a long time."

There was a long pause, filled with a hodgepodge of things like anxiety, low self-esteem, and loneliness. Angela was a mixed bag of unresolved issues, and she hung them all on a giant hook labeled 'Men'.

"Do you think that is why he likes me?"

"Don't jump to any conclusions yet. We don't even know if he knows who you are. He doesn't even know your last name, correct?"

"He knows me as Angie."

It wasn't much but it was something. I took a deep breath before I hit her with my next question.

"Where were you yesterday morning?"

"I went to Mykonos to get my hair done."

I stifled a smile. Everyone except Angela believed the local stylists were good enough. Tease (the local salon used the English word) was high-end, overpriced, and always twisted your arm until you left with a little paper bag filled with styling products. Tease catered to the Angelas of the island, wealthy tourists, and anyone else who could scrape together the small fortune one of their cuts cost. So I found it amusing that Tease wasn't good enough for Angela.

"Did you take the ferry?"

"Of course not!" She sounded offended. "I took one of my yachts."

Angela's name wasn't on Kyrios Harry's suspect list, but her bakery was run by a man who occupied a spot near the top. Call it me wanting to preemptively clear her name, I promised to let her know if and when Johnny rowed ashore, and then I went in search of the man who captained Angela's yachts to make sure the Mykonos story was true.

I wandered down to the dock and talked to Angela's captain, a young guy who defined the word "perky," and he confirmed what Angela had told me. They'd spend the morning and part of the afternoon, sailing to Mykonos and back.

My blood pressure sat back down, grabbed a newspaper, relaxed. Angela wasn't Harry's (or anyone else's) killer. I didn't think she was, but you never know with people. They do funny things if you put them in the corner.

Then he shook his head and squinted. "Wait—which one is Mykonos?"

Oh boy. Maybe he had a big brain, but it wasn't the one in his skull.

"Mykonos is the island south of here." Informative enough? Probably not. "If you look at a map, south is down." I pointed at the ground, just in case he wasn't familiar with the dictionary definition.

The lights in his head were on a dimmer switch. They came on slowly. "We went up, to the other island. I get names and directions mixed up. It's my dyslexia."

Yeah, I didn't think dyslexia was his problem. "Do you mean Skiathos?"

"Is that the one with the little island in the harbor?"

Maragos. He meant the islet of Maragos. Skiathos had a bunch of tiny satellites. Maragos was the one snuggled in the larger island's harbor.

"Yes."

"Then that's where we went!" He said it proudly, like he was a three-year-old who'd made it to the potty in time.

I thanked him for his time, then, with an icky feeling in my stomach, I trudged back to get my bicycle.

Angela couldn't be a killer.

But then that's what I'd thought about *Kyria* Kefala . And

look at her; that crafty old witch with her fake Alzheimer's had murdered my friend.

At the end of the dock there was a small commotion. The rescue boats were clustered together. People were shouting. I spotted Leo, talking into his phone. He was headed in my direction, so I put my head down and pretended he was the Invisible Man.

"Allie," he called out. "Didn't you get my text message?"

Rats. He'd caught me. I stopped, pivoted on one foot, and hoped he wouldn't murder me.

"I've been busy."

"So have I," he said, coming to a full halt in front of me. He glanced over one shoulder then swung back around. We've got a survivor."

CHAPTER SEVEN

"So you going to tell me how you knew?"

I played dumb. "Knew what?"

"That we were missing a person."

"I said you were missing a body, not a living person."

"You said I was missing one. That could be living or dead."

He had me there. "I told you: I used my powers of persuasion to get a headcount."

"Who is your source?"

"Who is the survivor?"

"No idea. Survivor is a woman. She's badly burned but still alive. Are you going to tell me who your source is?"

"No," I said simply. "Can I see her?"

"Why?"

"Curiosity."

He blew out a long sigh. "Nobody who isn't medical personal or law enforcement is going anywhere near her for a while. She's in bad shape. We might still lose her."

Lights and sirens blaring, an ambulance was trundling down the narrow road that connected to the dock. It rolled toward the rescue boats. The paramedics loaded their human cargo, then backed up slowly. Leo and I watched. We weren't the only ones. Everyone in the village had gravitated to the scene. Nobody wanted to miss out on this newsworthy moment.

They weren't all civilians.

Merope Fores—the Merope Times—was the island's one and only newspaper. The newspaper had been in the family since Merope scored a name and inhabitants worth writing about. The Bakas family rarely hired outsiders, professionally or maritally. Their family tree was a straight stick. The latest puddle of sap was standing ten feet away from us, notepad in hand, eyes on the departing ambulance. When it vanished out of sight, his head swiveled and his gaze landed on Leo with an almost audible *thunk*.

"Who is in the ambulance?"

"Poseidon's *poutsa*," Leo said.

I stuffed my laugh back down my throat. If even a squeak popped out, I would be all over the paper tomorrow, painted as a callous *skeela*, laughing at burn victims.

"Time to run," I said.

"Wait," Leo said. "We need to talk."

"You know where I live." I pointed two finger guns at him and fired.

I knew where I lived, too, which is why I rode straight home. Lunchtime had snuck up on me, and now my stomach was voicing its displeasure. It really wanted a sandwich, and so did the rest of me.

Kyrios Yiannis, the dead gardener, was busy pruning the courtyard's bushes. He raised his hand and waved to me as I approached.

"Someone is here to see you," he said.

"What kind of someone?" I held my phone to my ear so

no one would inspect me for missing screws if they witnessed my conversation with thin air.

"A man."

"What does he look like?"

He stopped clipping for a moment to shrug. "A man."

"Thanks for nothing."

"*Parakalo*," he answered without a shred of sarcasm, and went back to his fruitless work.

Parakalo is one of those words that pulls double duty. It's "please" and "you're welcome".

Curiosity piqued, I jogged upstairs. My visitor was standing outside my apartment, staring out the hallway's picture window. His back was to me but I recognized the long black coat and the blacker than night boots. At the nape, his dark hair curled, touching the coat's collar. During our first encounter I established that he exuded cool and that his voice evoked memories of ancient and unsolved mysteries, foreign, unexplored places, and candlelight. The mysterious man would have been right at home in a Jane Austen novel. At first I'd mistaken him for a ghost, but he was solid and could interact with me and the world around us. No falling through walls and chairs for this guy, whatever he was. His body was hard and well-built. I didn't know who he was—all I knew is that he came and went and sometimes our paths crossed. This was the first time he'd sought me out at home.

My voice crackled on its way out. "Are you looking for me?"

He turned slowly, a frown unfurling across his face. His eyes were shrouded with shadows that didn't seem native to the hallway. "Yes."

I raised both my arms. "Here I am."

"Not all apparitions belong to the dead," he said in that hypnotic voice. That melodic sound, I could listen to him for hours. A fireplace would be involved, and a comfortable chair, and rugs and paintings from another century. There would be crusty rustic loaves in a wooden bowl, and for some reason, grapes.

He moved closer and the shadow dissipated. His dark eyes held mine. I was paralyzed ... until he walked past me and kept on going. Shocked, I turned around.

"Wait, you're leaving?"

He stopped. "I'll find you again, if you need me."

"Are you some kind of guardian angel?"

He smiled. "I am no angel."

Then he continued down the hall until the stairs carried him away. I exhaled long and deep and stood in the hallway, thinking.

What he'd said resonated with me. I had more ghosts in my apartment than the morgue had dead people from the Royal Pain's wreck. If everyone in my apartment was dead, then either a body was still missing, or someone was tagging along for the ride.

But who?

There was no way to ask Detective Samaras to take a picture of the lone survivor without arousing more of his curiosity and suspicion. After our date, he already thought I was a whacko, which is rich coming from a potential serial killer. Maybe I could convince Constable Pappas to sneak in and snap a photo. Or someone else. Merope was small enough that I knew everyone's faces and most of their names. Things didn't get anonymous until summer struck and the island's population exploded.

I made a quick call to one of the nurses I knew. We'd gone to school together, and she was a reliable source of information.

"They're not letting anyone in except doctors and two nurses at the moment," she told me apologetically. "The police have her room locked down tight. Nobody goes in without their permission. They're saying she murdered all those people on that yacht."

"The police are saying that?"

"No. But everyone else is. Why else would they keep us out unless she committed a crime?"

It was a good point ... for something that was based on nothing. I thanked her, ended the call, and prepared to bust some ghosts.

In I went.

The ghosts were home—all seven of them. The women-folk were crowded around the TV—still. Harry was at the window—still.

"Okay," I said. "One of you spooks is not a ghost. Who is it?"

The older woman I'd taken for Kyria Vasilikos, Harry's wife, slowly stood and turned to face me.

"That would be me."

———

Two minutes later, we were both pacing.

"I don't know," the not-a-ghost said. "I promise. We were eating lunch, then we were here. When we first came to your apartment I thought I was dead like the others. Then I real-ized there was no light for me, no waiting room in the After-life. I was on the boat, then I was in your apartment. There was nothing in between."

"The rest of you went to the Afterlife first, yes?" I asked the others.

One at the time, the yeses came back to me.

"The waiting room, yes," Kyrios Harry said.

"You can all see her?" I pointed to the woman, whose name I didn't know. "What's your name? In my head you're still *Kyria* Vasiliko, even though you're not his wife."

"Eva. My name is Eva Vasiliko."

"Not his wife though?" I gestured at *Kyrios* Harry, who looked horrified at the idea.

"Sister," he said.

I tried to imagine sailing the seas with Toula. No way. Couldn't do it. Eventually I'd be driven to toss one of us overboard. Would that be murder or self-preservation?

Or murder as self-preservation?

"Everyone else onboard died, but not you," I said to Eva Vasiliko. "Why not? Don't get me wrong, I'm glad you're alive, but why you and not the others?"

We paced some more, the transparent woman and me.

I stopped. Faced her. "What did you eat? More importantly, what didn't you eat?"

She shrugged. "I ate what everyone else was eating. That morning it was fruits and cheeses."

More pacing happened. A lot of it. *Kyria* Eva was bird thin. Blow on her wrists and they'd snap like crackers. Difficult to imagine her eating anything. There is naturally thin, then there's a thinness that comes from years of deprivation dieting. *Kyria* Eva's face was gaunt. Her bones were missing a layer of padding. She looked like something the dog dragged out and shook until the stuffing was history. Fruits. Cheeses. Fruits. Cheeses. Something was missing—something Greek.

"What about bread? Did you eat bread?"

A Greek who didn't eat bread. That didn't compute. Bread is the cornerstone of the Greek diet. It's their food, it's their knife. Bread was at that table, guaranteed.

Kyria Eva shuddered. "There was bread."

"But did you eat it?"

"I never eat bread."

"Low carb diet?"

"Bread makes you fat. Look at them."

She was talking about the dead women, every one of them

on the high end of underweight. If bread did that, every woman in the western world would be mainlining toast.

"So they're dead and you're not, and you're the only one who shunned the bread." Not a question; I was clarifying things for myself.

Kyrios Harry chose that moment to interrupt. "You think somebody poisoned my bread?"

"Your bread?"

"Royal Pain bread."

I stopped again. "You were serving Royal Pain bread on the yacht?"

Two palms up. "What else? My bread is the best bread in Greece."

Somehow I doubted that. I remembered Penny Papadopoulo's words, particularly how many times she used "*skata*" in reference to Kyrios Harry and his bread.

"To answer your question, yes, if you were poisoned, it's possible that the bread—your bread—was the vehicle for that poison. Which means it could have been poisoned any time." I flopped down in my office chair and opened my laptop's lid. Interesting that the murderer had chosen to poison the bread. They were really sticking it to Harry Vasilikos, killing him with his own product. Maybe everyone else was probably collateral damage—everyone except *Kyrios* Harry's sister. Her diet had saved her life.

But if she was alive, why was she here, and how? Ghosts were basically souls that had permanently left the building. Maybe they could take vacations if the body and brain were banged up enough. Leo mentioned that the survivor was in critical condition. Probably she was unconscious.

One survivor. Six dead. Luck or design? Was Eva Vasiliko the murderer? I ran the scenario in my head but the ending didn't fit. Why kill *Kyrios* Harry and the others, then sit back as the yacht plowed into an island?

"If you didn't eat the bread, why didn't you call for help or manually override the yacht?"

"I don't know." She wrapped her arms around her body, hugged her thin bones tight. "Maybe I tried. I don't remember."

Could be the crash was affecting her memory.

For the moment, I added Kyria Eva to the suspect list, right at the tippy top.

Kyrios Harry peered over my shoulder. "Why is my sister on the list?" he said in the snotty tone of someone who thinks they poop rainbows and candy.

"Because she's alive and you're not."

He did some quick math in his transparent head. "You think she poisoned the bread?"

Kyria Eva crossed herself, then clutched the xylophone that passed for her chest with a red-tipped claw. "I would never murder my own brother. Them," she nodded to the bikini-clad entourage "maybe, but only because they are strangers and not very clever ones. But I did not murder them."

The gaggle of nearly identical women ignored her. My television was more captivating. Good thing they couldn't touch anything or they'd boost my phone to check their social media.

"Last time a murder fell in my lap, I made a wrong call. She's on the list because if there's one thing I know about people, it's that you never really know people."

"So cynical," *Kyria* Eva said.

"Not always," I said. "I'm a happy drunk."

On that note, I saved the revised document, went to my kitchen, cobbled together a simple sandwich—*kaseri* cheese, salami, and bread. No mustard. No mayo. I eyed the bread with suspicion, then bit into it anyway because it wasn't a Royal Pain loaf.

What if the Vasilikos murders were unlucky accidents and not a murders at all?

I dropped the sandwich back onto the plate.

Leo. I wanted to call him. Needed to call him. Virgin Mary, why did he have to be a potential serial killer? Why couldn't he just be some normal guy who'd boned my sister back in high school? That I could deal with. Being maybe murdered in my sleep was a no-go.

No. My parents didn't raise a pair of fools.

Instead of calling Leo, I hit the internet and ran a search for recent deaths in Greece. I was looking for unsolved cases, mysterious deaths, poisonings, that sort of thing.

"What are you doing now?" *Kyrios* Harry asked me. He was peering over my shoulder. Again. The way he did personal space, he'd be comfortable in Tokyo.

"What does it look like I'm doing?"

"Browsing obituaries. Why?"

"It's what I do for fun," I lied.

He moved away. "You are a strange woman."

Pretty rich, coming from a ghost. "I want to know if you're the only ones who were poisoned by Royal Pain bread. Maybe you weren't an isolated case."

Here came his nose, poking over my shoulder again, reading my screen. "Are you saying someone sabotaged my factories?"

"No. I'm saying I want to know *if* someone sabotaged your factories."

"Wundebar Bread," he muttered.

"I haven't ruled that out. Thanassi Dalaras died but—"

"His widow lives here on Merope, but I do not know if she still owns the company."

"She wasn't on your list." Angela was on mine though, written in invisible, imaginary ink.

"Angela does not have a mean bone in her body, just a lot of stupid ones."

Was that a glowing endorsement or not? I couldn't tell.

I didn't tell him Angela still owned the company. For now, let him think of Johnny Margas as the company's frontman and suspect—at least until I had a chance to confront Angela. "Wait," I said. "Do you know Yiannis Margas personally?"

"We were friends."

"Before you died?"

"Before he *hezo*'d on our friendship. We were in the navy together when we were young."

"So he's old like you?"

"I am not old!"

"That's right, you're dead. You're not anything anymore."

Mean, yes. But Harry Vasilikos's ghost was breathing down my neck and reading over my shoulder. I couldn't elbow him in the face so I had to rely on sarcasm and cutting remarks.

"Death is not the worst thing that has ever happened to me," he said.

Yikes. I almost felt bad for the man. "What happened between you and Margas?"

"He went to work for Thanassi Dalaras at Wundebar Bread, after I offered him a job."

"If you were friends, why didn't he take the job."

Kyrios Harry's sister jumped in. "Because the job my brother offered him was menial and beneath him. Thanassi Dalaras offered him work that let him be a man."

Charming woman, that Eva Vasiliko. The type who looked down on the people who waited on her hand and foot.

I pulled up the picture Angela had· given me of her new beau. He was attractive if you had a thing for reptiles and oil spills. Angela had two types, and those types were Filthy Rich and Bad to the Boner. I didn't mention that Angela and Johnny Margas were embroiled in a long-distance fling.

"Is this Yiannis Margas?"

Harry looked and laughed "Sure. Maybe twenty, thirty years ago."

A-ha! So the guy running Angela's bread business, weaseling his way into her life and possibly her treasure chest (not a euphemism; Angela actually owned a treasure chest) had shaved at least two decades off his age. Angela wouldn't be happy. She liked her Bad to the Boner types to come without a pillbox.

Now I had two reasons to pedal over to Angela's villa. But I couldn't go without proof. Angela would laugh me out of the house if I told her a ghost had tattled on her sweetheart. The internet wasn't any help, either. Some weirdoes aren't on social media. I was one of them. My business was, but not my face. Johnny Margas wasn't anywhere else on the internet either, not as a face. His name was sprinkled here and there in connection with the bread business, but otherwise, he was a ghost. Figuratively.

Angela had asked me to verify his good looks. No mention of wanting to know his age or other statistics. Time to go digging a little deeper on Johnny Margas.

I shot Sam an email with Johnny's details—what few I had —and asked him to run a quick, detailed search.

Sam called me. "What do you think I am, a wizard?"

"Yes."

He laughed. "You've got that right. Hold tight."

While Sam was working his wizard magic, I grabbed my sandwich and wrapped it in a napkin. Into my bag it went.

"Where are you going now?" *Kyrios* Harry wanted to know.

"I've never had a mother-in-law," I said, "but if I had a really nosy, bossy one, she'd be just like you." I slung my bag across my body, took a step toward the front door, then stopped. A thought had just popped into my head. With the whole Leo thing messing with my head, I was slacking. The question should have been my first.

"*Kyrios* Harry, who inherits everything now that you're dead?"

"The business goes to my sister. My art collection goes to various galleries."

"You collect art?"

"Paintings of bread," *Kyria* Eva said dryly.

"Paintings with bread in them," her brother clarified. "The bread does not have to be the main feature. There is very little art where bread is the subject."

Everyone collected something, I supposed. Rich people could afford to indulge their quirks more often and more easily than the rest of us. "What about your money?"

"Donated to a good cause," Harry said.

"Medical research? Hungry children? Homeless veterans? Sad puppies?"

"Politics."

So, not a good cause then. I made mental note and headed for the door. While I was waiting on Sam, I figured I had time to make a house call. But before I could yank the door open, there was a scuffling on the other side, then a knock.

I peered through the spy hole.

Toula had come calling.

Normally my sister dressed like she was three-quarters Amish. She didn't believe in cleavage or things like skinny jeans. She liked scarves and buttons that went all the way up to where her chest became chin. From the neck up she was me. From the neck down, she was one belief system away from magic underwear. So I recoiled when today's fashion choice registered. Pajamas, with a cardigan thrown hastily over the top. Yikes. Was the world ending?

"Are you home?" she called out. "You must be. Your bicycle is downstairs."

I opened the door. "I'm on my way out. What's wrong?"

"I changed my mind. Take them. Please, take them. Otherwise I am going to bang their heads together like a pair of soft coconuts. What kind of mother would I be if I banged their heads together then spent the rest of my life in jail?"

I looked past her hip. The hallway was empty. "Where are they?"

"In the van. Will you take them?"

"I'm going to church."

"Perfect. Tell them to beg God for forgiveness while they're there."

"What did they do?"

"What didn't they do?" A noise at the end of the hall jerked her attention sideways. "I told you two to stay in the car."

Milos and Petra appeared at her elbow, grinning. Their hair was wild, their faces were sticky.

"Candy?" I asked Toula in English.

"More like Sandy."

Sandy is Toula's best friend, even after all these years away from the United States. They're a continent apart but their friendship is stretchy.

"Let me guess. She sent a care package."

"I don't know why she didn't just fill the box with high fructose corn syrup." She gave me a desperate look, like she was on the lam and needed a fake ID and new face to go with it. "The kids got to the box before I did. There was no time to hide it."

I winced. "How much did they eat?"

"All of it. All. Of. It. I was in the bathroom watching *Outlander* on my phone. I didn't hear a thing. They were so quiet."

No wonder my niece and nephew were practically levitating. All that sugar, and now Toula wanted to pass their sugar high to me.

"No problem," I said. One of Toula's favorite hobbies was bossing me around, but she was still my sister, and she was always there when I needed her.

The munchkins shot past my legs and pressed their sugar against my sofa. Patra, the six-year-old sat up and looked at us.

"A whale's *poutsa* is bigger than your apartment," she said. "That's what Mama told us."

"I did not," Toula said.

Milos was on his sister's side. "Yes, you did."

"What's a *poutsa*?" Patra asked.

"More trouble than it's worth," Toula said.

The ghosts, and *Kyria* Eva's apparition, were happily watching my family sitcom unfold.

"This is better than television," one of the bikini girl said.

Kyrios Harry had put on a smirk for the occasion. "Even your sister and her family are a disaster."

It takes a special kind of person to block out the dead while socializing with the living, and I am not that kind of person. I scratched the side of my nose with my raised middle finger, hoping Toula wouldn't catch me and that Kyrios Harry and his *companions* would get the message.

"A whale's everything is bigger than my apartment, but that's okay," I told my nephew and niece. "As long as I don't buy a pet whale, I'm safe."

Patra giggled. She smeared a hand across her sticky face. Oh boy.

"Go," I told Toula, before I changed my mind. "I'll get them cleaned up and then take them to repent their sins."

"What are sins?" Patra wanted to know.

"Things like opening packages addressed to your mother," I told her.

The tiny girl nodded solemnly. "Then we definitely did sins."

"I would have opened the box, too," I said in a loud whisper.

"Allie!" Toula barked. But she looked less bedraggled and stressed already. "I'll leave you the van. I can walk home."

"Forget it," I said. "You're in your pajamas. Besides, the walk will do them good. They can burn off some of that sugar."

———

"Are we there yet?"

"No."

"How about now?"

"No."

"Now?"

Milos and Patra giggled. "Why do you keep asking that?" Milos asked.

I sighed like the walk was killing me. They giggled again. "Because usually I ride all over Merope. All this walking is hard work."

It wasn't really. Riding kept me at a decent level of fitness. I could eat cake without crying to the therapist I didn't have. But the kids were getting a kick out of my dramatic complaining, so I hammed it up and added some dawdling to the mix.

We came to the main road. Vasilis Moustakas waved the moment he spotted me with the kids. "I had sex with your *yiayia*," he called out.

The kids couldn't see him or hear him but I covered their ears anyway.

Patra looked up at me. "What are you doing, *Thea* Allie?"

"I need new ears. I'm trying to figure out if yours will fit."

————

God's house. That's what a church is supposed to be. The way *Kyria* Sofia swanned around *Ayios* Konstantinos, you'd think it was her house. She was currently dishing out orders to the church's caretaker, *Kyria* Aspasia. *Kyria* Aspasia had a humped spine, eighty years in her past, and one eye. She was using the latter to look for dirt that wasn't there. I knew where the dirt was: all over the priest's sister.

"Aliki Callas," Kyria Sofia cried out, rushing to greet me. She air-kissed me on both cheeks, and now I knew what it was like to be kissed by a spider. "Twice in one day. Have you come to pray for your immortal soul?" Her gaze skated sideways as my niece and nephew zipped past her and plonked themselves down on the ground alongside *Kyria* Aspasia.

"I saw you in that movie," Milos said to the hunched over woman.

"A scary movie," said his sister, wide-eyed. They were both looking at that hump like it was its own entity. "There was a big church, a mean man, and real pretty girl."

"And talking gargoyles," Milos said. "They were funny."

Beside me, *Kyria* Sofia gasped like she didn't have a hard drive full of animal porn.

I raised my eyebrows in their direction. "Milos, Patra. Be polite."

The old caretaker was unfazed. "My hump is full of secrets," she said slyly.

Those wide eyes widened, until their faces were mostly eyeballs. "What secrets?" Milos asked.

"If I tell you they would not be secrets." *Kyria* Aspasia

kept sweeping. "You can only see them if you have one eye, like me."

"I want to have one eye when I grow up," Patra said.

My nephew had other ideas. "If you want, I can poke your eye out now. Which one do you want to keep?"

The old woman nudged his foot with her broom. "You cannot see my hump's secrets if someone pokes out your eye on purpose. You must lose the eye in battle."

"A battle with what?" Milos asked.

Kyria Aspasia had the situation under control, which left me free to deal with the priest's sister.

"I just have some questions," I asked *Kyria* Sofia.

Kyria Prim and Not-Even-Remotely Proper touched the ladybug brooch at her throat. "For me?"

The way to the vault inside *Kyria* Sofia's head was through her ego, and I was not above stroking it a little. Flattery won't get you everywhere in life, but it opens a lot of closed doors.

"You know everyone on Merope, and you know every-thing there is to know. People trust you and they like you." The way they trust and like snakes.

"That is true," she said without a trace of irony. "How can I help you, my girl?"

"You mentioned Harry Vasilikos used to come to Merope often."

"That was a long time ago. Why do you want to know?"

The lie came easily enough. As far as lies went, it was benign. "A client of mine is writing a book about Greek millionaires, including Harry Vasilikos."

Her eyes lit up. "Is this client from Merope?"

"I can't say. It's confidential."

She fiddled with the ladybug. "I understand." Her face said she did not understand any such thing and she thought I was rotten for keeping secrets from her. "There was a picture of us together in the newspaper. Did you see it?"

There was a picture of *Kyria* Sofia and every notable person to ever stop foot on Merope in the paper, sooner or later. In the USA, they would call her a star-fucker or an attention-whore. I didn't mention that "a long time" ago I was just a kid in another country, therefore I didn't see that particular issue of the *Merope Fores*, but I did make a polite noise and tell her I wished I had seen it.

She took that as a sign of encouragement. "Today is a lucky one because I have it right here. Let me find it for you." She whipped out her fancy phone and swiped until she and Harry Vasilikos were on the screen, arms around each other, both grinning. They were both younger, and Harry was still alive.

"In those days he used to have the most wonderful dog," she said. "A big German shepherd. That dog would do anything for a treat."

My eye twitched. "Was *Kyrios* Vasilikos well-liked?"

"Of course. He was rich."

"Did he have other friends on Merope? Colleagues? Acquaintances?"

"Let me think." She looped her arm through mine and casually steered me toward the large and ostentatious candle holder. It was filled with sand to hold the thin beeswax candles upright while they burned. People lit them for the dead, and sometimes for those they wished were dead. Greek people are simpler and more complicated than most.

We weren't here for the candles though. The parts of *Kyria* Sofia that were not motivated by prestige or cute animals were motivated by cold, hard cash. Or soft, floppy checks—cheques if you're British. Next to the candle holder stood a gilt table, and upon it a large wooden box with a brass latch and matching padlock. The wood was something dark and expensive, polished to a mirror-like shine. In the top was a slot. A giant piggy bank. *Kyria* Sofia was only too happy to help ... for a price.

"This is a good place to think," she said.

I could take a hint, especially when she was rubbing my face in it. Out of my purse came a twenty-euro note, in blues and featuring stained glass windows. I folded it in half and pushed it through the slot.

Kyria Sofia made a soft, satisfied sound. "You are too generous."

"If you like I can swap it for a ten."

She patted my arm. "Twenty will be fine. Now that I think about it, Harry was good friends with Angela Zouboulaki and her first husband." Her eyes sparkled almost as much as the church's gold accents. "I bet she even met his dog."

———

After the church, Sam still wasn't done digging up the goods on Johnny Margas, so I took the kids to the playground next to *Ayios* Konstatinos.

Toula called. "Are they still alive?"

I played dumb. "Who?"

Tense silence.

"Relax," I said. "We're at the playground."

"Which playground?"

"The one by the church. Why?

Relieved sigh. "Have they killed anyone yet?"

"No, but they asked *Kyria* Aspasia about her hump."

"Did she tell them it was filled with secrets?"

"How did you know?"

"Because her hump is filled with secrets."

Something moved out of the corner of my eye. A yacht was coming in to port. I grabbed the small pair of binoculars I kept in my bag for snooping emergencies. Nice boat. Big, but not Royal Pain big. I watched it slow down and angle its large body until it was snugged up to the dock. On the deck, a man was waiting. Blue blazer. Gold buttons. White pants. Silly hat. What was it with these old guys and their nautical uniforms? Didn't they know you could wear regular clothes on a yacht? Women did it all the time.

The man's sagging face was instantly recognizable, even with an extra twenty years etched on his skin.

I pulled out my phone and made a call. "Angela? Here's Johnny."

CHAPTER EIGHT

"What," Angela said, "are these?"

Milos and Patra were bouncing around behind me, pretending to be *My Little Ponies*. Patra was Pinkie Pie, and Milos was some pony called Dog Fart. I didn't think Dog Fart was a real pony name, but you never know with kids' shows these days. Maybe they were aggressively and openly chasing the brony market now.

"They're my sister's."

"And you want to bring them into my house?"

Angela does not live in a house. Mansion is the correct word. A hulking white structure with an ocean view, although technically, the Aegean Sea is a sea. The word is right there in the name. Even more technically, the Aegean Sea is an embayment of the Mediterranean Sea (also not an ocean), so there is no ocean involved in Angela's view whatsoever. Everything about the property is white or chrome. The mansion. The geometric fountains. The smooth, concrete grounds. Everything inside the house, except a single painting in one of her living rooms. Angela lives in a laboratory designed by an obsessive compulsive Scandinavian. Warmth visits Angela's house to die. This was exactly where you wanted to be during August.

"We can talk out here," I assured her.

She visibly relaxed. As always, Angela was freshly coiffed, her face recently dipped in a bucket of no-makeup makeup. Her age is a secret. But I caught a glimpse of her real face once, between Botox shots and chemical peels, and I'd guessed she was in her sixth decade. She's slim and dresses well. Today she was in dove gray slacks and a turtleneck sweater that looked like it was made from some kind of soft, rare animal fleece. Angela is plain but she uses her money to paint a prettier portrait over the canvas.

"You said Johnny is here. Did you see him? Is he handsome or is he a lying *poutsokleftis*?"

I didn't know if Johnny was a dick thief or not and told her so. "How old did he say he was?"

"Forty-five. Why?"

I shoved my hands into my pockets and looked back to make sure the kids weren't choking each other. They were both alive. Good.

"He's older."

Her voice turned to steel that had spent several winters in Antarctica with the penguins. "How much older?"

"About twenty years."

"A good sixty-five or a bad sixty-five?"

"Have you ever left a leather bag out in the rain then tried to blow it dry with a hairdryer?"

"No."

"Have you ever left vegetables too long in the back of the refrigerator?"

"I never touch the refrigerator. That is what servants are for."

Sometimes Angela did not live on the same planet as regular people.

I opened my bag, ripped a piece of paper out my notepad, scrunched it between my hands until it was a wrinkled mess, then offered it to her.

She arched a thin eyebrow. "What is that?"

"Johnny Margas's face."

Blood vacating her complexion, she braced herself against the doorframe with one hand and clutched her chest with the other. "Allie, tell me, what am I going to do?"

"You could try not answering the door."

"I never answer my own door."

"Tell your butler not to open the door."

Tears burst out of her like an Alien through a chest. Her makeup was unaffected by the sudden deluge. "Why does this always happen to me?" she wailed. "Why do men always turn out to be hideous, deformed monsters or cheating *malakes*? What is wrong with them?"

I grabbed a tissue out of my bag and delicately dabbed around her eyes. This wasn't the first time I'd had to mop up her tears. One more time and I would be able to list it as a skill on my resume—if I ever needed a resume.

"I wouldn't called Johnny deformed, just older than forty-five."

"Sixty-five! That is twenty years older than me!"

Not on any of the world's numeral systems. "I'm sure there's a decent man out there for you. One your own age." *Cough, cough.* "Just be patient."

She sniffled. "You have to do something."

Uh-oh. "What kind of something?"

"Get rid of him."

An image popped into my head: me whacking Johnny over the head with a skillet and shoving him off a cliff, while Angela cheered.

"You know I'm not an assassin, right?"

Her tears dried up. "I thought you did everything."

"No. I find things, information, and sometimes people."

"Oh." She sounded disappointed for a moment, then she brightened up. "Can you find me an assassin?"

"Also, no."

"Okay. Then you will have to tell him to go away."

My eyebrows went for a short hike. "You want me to dump him for you?"

"Yes. I will pay you. How much do you charge to dump boyfriends who lied about their age?"

"I don't. I find things."

She threw out a figure that made my eyebrows hike another inch.

"Well, I guess now I find things *and* dump boyfriends who lie about their age," I said.

"Good." She made a little "shoo" gesture. "Do it today. And make sure you take those with you."

She meant Pinkie Pie and Dog Fart, who were silently contemplating a fountain that, from this angle, resembled two romantically entwined dogs.

"That looks like Mama and Baba," Patra said.

Milos nodded. "Every Saturday night."

———

Dumping men wasn't my forte. Was there some kind of protocol? Could I text Johnny to deliver the bad news? No, that was cruel. Login to Angela's social media and unfollow him on everything? No, too millennial.

"How do you dump men?" I asked Lydia, who was easing through the apartment building's door in a pair of lethal plat-form heels and hot pants with camel toe. I knew I was getting older because I wanted to tell her to put on a coat before she got a chill.

Milos stared at her, mouth open. Now the kid was going

to grow up with issues. Probably he'd wind up being shoe fetish serial killer like Jerry Brudos. Thinking about serial killers made me think about Leo, whose car was parked at the curb. Was he killing someone right now? No, I would hear that kind of commotion through the ceiling.

When Leo first moved in, I had mistaken him for a hump-happy playboy, with a revolving bedroom door. Then I realized the guy worked out at home. Noise definitely traveled, despite decent insulation. If he murdered someone upstairs there would be no missing the flailing and the cries for help.

Lydia was staring at me with a curious and amused expression. "I didn't realize you were seeing someone."

"It's not for me."

"Friend?"

"Client." I didn't mention the about-to-be-dumped individual was Johnny Margas.

"I hope they're paying you well."

"Very well, so I need it to be good."

Lydia shrugged prettily. "I ghost them."

Was this a murder thing? "Ghost them?"

"When they call, I don't call back. I vanish ..." she performed a move a lot like jazz hands "...like a ghost."

I filed that one away in my memory banks. "I think my client wants me to be more active, so there's no confusion."

"What's the reason for the breakup?"

When I told her she made a face. "That happened to me once. He shaved ten years off his age."

"What did you do?"

She grinned, full and red. Probably her lipstick never smudged. "I go to Athens and give him a *tsibouki* every other month."

I slapped my hands over Patra and Milos's ears. "You didn't break up with him?"

"There are worse things a person can lie about." She winked at the gawking Milos, then stalked off into the night. All three of us watched her leave; we couldn't help ourselves. Lydia was compelling.

"Is she a *putana*?" Milos wanted to know.

"No, she's just young and pretty."

Patra looked up at me. "What's a *putana*?"

"Better than a politician, that's what." I steered them toward the door before the questions gained momentum.

There was a noise behind us. Leaves rustling. Then: "Is she gone?"

I looked around. The words were coming from the bushes. "Who?"

"Lydia, the goddess."

I groaned as Jimmy Kontos emerged from the bushes. His beard had twigs. His skin was scratched. A dopey, love-struck look was stuck to his face.

"Were you hiding from her?"

"I didn't want her to see me like this," he said. Jimmy was in his Ugg boots and cutoff sweats.

"Like what? Short? Newsflash: she knows you're a *nanos*."

"Stupid giant." He took off down the sidewalk, muttering.

At my side, Patra was wide-eyed. "*Thea* Allie, was that Rumpelstiltskin?"

"I heard that," Jimmy called out.

"Yes," I said, "and he's going to spin *kaka* into more *kaka*."

Toula's children giggled.

"I heard that, too!"

————

Dumping Johnny would have to wait. These children needed their food and their mother, and not in that order. Toula showed up as I was scanning my kitchen cupboards, wondering if coffee and Merenda sandwiches were a valid food groups for people under the age of sixteen. She bundled up her drooping children, and we herded them back to her minivan, one of the few on the island. Then we stood on the road, jiggling to stay warm. Finally we had privacy, so I could ask her something.

"Leo said you went to see him."

Her eyes cut from me to the street, and they stayed there. Decades of being her sister told me that Toula's pants were about to self-combust. "It's a small island. Eventually everyone talks to everyone."

No way was I going to let her off that easily. Not *my* sister. "Oh, no, no. We're not talking a casual meeting in the street. You went to see him at work."

"Sometimes I hate this place." She lowered her voice. "Okay, I went to see him. But don't say anything to Kostas. Please?"

Kostas is her husband. My brother-in-law is directly responsible for half of his children's DNA—probably the part that makes up names like Dog Fart. Together they own a business called Go Car Go, which—spoiler alert—fixes cars.

"What's going on, Toula?"

"You wouldn't understand."

"Try me."

"Is it true you went on a date with Leo?"

Very stealthy, the way she changed the subject. It worked, darn it. "Half a date. No—not even half a date. I'm not sure anyone could even call it a date. I don't. It was more of a comedy of errors."

Her eyes lit up with curiosity. Her expression shifted into motherly and nurturing mode. "What happened?"

"No big deal. It just isn't meant to be, that's all."

Silence—from her and from me. Then: "Are you going to tell me why you went to see Leo?"

"Thanks," she said, swinging around to look at the mini-van. "I mean it."

Toula was keeping secrets. That made two of us.

"Any time."

Toula hugged me and left me to my ghosts and my head full of questions.

My phone rang as I was settling down at my desk.

"Did you tell him yet?" Angela wanted to know. "Did he cry?"

"Not yet. I'm on my way."

"Make it something awful. I want him to hurt the way he hurt me. And if he cries, take pictures so I can enjoy them."

Yikes. I promised pain and tears, then got rid of her so I could hunt down Johnny Margas.

Kyrios Harry was listening in again. The ghost was a real snoop. "If you are looking for Johnny he will be on his yacht. He never sleeps anywhere except his own beds."

"Why not?"

"Everyone in his family has died in a bed that was not theirs. He believes if he always sleeps in his own bed he can cheat death."

Cum hoc ergo propter hoc. With this, therefore because of this. Also known as the "correlation proves causation" fallacy. Everyone died in a strange bed, therefore the strange bed was the cause of death. Greeks loves that one. It dovetails nicely with their penchant for superstitions.

"Is there anything else you can tell me about Johnny Margas?"

My email pinged. Incoming from Sam, at last. I scanned the email, then smiled. My gaze slid sideways, to where *Kyria* Eva was sitting primly on my couch with the stick firmly lodged between her bony cheeks. Was it my imagination or was she eavesdropping?

"Never mind," I said. "I've got more than I need."

Johnny Margas's yacht was nice. Too bad it wasn't his yacht.

"I like your boat," I said.

Yiannis "Johnny" Margas didn't flinch, twitch, or correct me. Instead, he scraped his gaze all over me, leaving my skin and clothes covered in a thin, invisible coat of oil. "*Kalipsera*," he said, wishing me a good evening in what was supposed to be an inviting, seductive voice.

Didn't work on me. Not a fan of reptiles. "Are you *Kyrios* Margas?"

Smirk. "You can call me Johnny. Do you have a name or should I just call you Beautiful?"

He much too old to be this greasy, in his silly nautical costume, with his ridiculous hat.

"Aliki Callas." I didn't waste time. "Angela Zouboulaki sent me to speak with you."

His smile melted to half mast. His eyes darted right then left. This was a man recalculating his odds and realizing they weren't about to favor him. "She cannot talk to me herself?"

"She doesn't want to."

"Why not?"

"Because you're a lying liar who lies. You told her you were forty-five."

"Oh. That." He shrugged. "Everybody lies."

"Yes, but not usually about everything."

Left and right, left and right. This guy really didn't want to be overheard.

"What do you mean?"

"Oh, I think you know. Should we talk about who owns this boat? I bet Angela doesn't know."

The remnants of his smile fell away. "Come aboard." His tone had grit now. Less oil. "We can talk inside, where it is private."

That wasn't going to happen. My grandmother always gave advice—not always good advice, but definitely advice. Like, "If a man wants to spank you say yes, because afterwards he will give you money or dinner—both if you are lucky," and, "Never wear clean underwear on a date because if you lose your underwear you will save yourself some laundry." She also told me to never get on boats with rich strangers because rich men can afford to sail away and dump your body at sea.

"We don't have to talk. I just need you to listen. Angela doesn't want to see you because you lied to her. But," I said, "your wife is in the hospital here, so you should probably visit her."

His face paled. "Eva is here?"

"She was in an accident." I gave him a quick rundown of the tragedy that befell Harry Vasilikos and the Royal Pain.

"And she is alive?"

"Barely."

"Thank the Virgin Mary!"

Was he happy she was alive or happy she was barely alive? Hard to say.

I pointed my finger at him. It had an accusatory tip. "Stay away from Angela." Then I managed a dignified half spin and walked away.

"Or what?" he called out after me.

I turned around, shrugged. "Or nothing. I'm just the messenger."

———

I was back at Angela's again, putting a smile on her face. We were in her white living room, sitting on white furniture. Dressed in black, I felt like a stain.

"Tell me again," Angela said. "Only this time do it with actions."

Once more, with feeling and actions.

She bit her lacquered lip in its tasteful pink shade. "I was hoping for more pain and a lot of man-tears, but I suppose this will do."

"I uncovered dirt and flung it in his face. That part was great."

"The last one was married, too."

"Divorced."

"Same thing."

Not even close. Last time she flipped out because the guy in question had been married once, years earlier, and hadn't bothered to mention it. He had actually loved Angela, but then he was murdered and that cut the relationship short.

"What now?" I asked her.

"Now I have to find somebody else."

I ventured out onto the thin ice. "Have you considered avoiding men for a while?"

Her eyebrows tried to rise but the Botox had her whole forehead in chains. "Words are coming out of your mouth but I do not understand what you are saying."

"Maybe be single for a while. Relax. Work on yourself." Yes, I'd take a pay hit but it would be worth it for Angela to get her life together.

"Work on myself ... Are you saying I need more plastic surgery?"

My Virgin Mary. "No. I'm saying stay away from men until you can pick a decent one."

Tears bubbled up in her eyes. "But they are all so awful."

"No, they're not. You're a magnet for bad ones, so take your time and find a good one."

"But that's why I have you," she said. "To figure out which ones are bad."

Something else had slipped into second position, behind the Johnny Margas issue. Angela had lied to me about her boat trip to Skiathos. I wanted to know why, especially when six people died not long after pulling out of that same port and one was in Merope's ICU.

When I mentioned her error, her gaze darted away and landed on the large painting of herself on the living room wall. The painting was the room's only color source.

"Skiathos, Mykonos, same thing," she said.

"Except they're in completely different directions."

"I had a thing."

"What kind of thing."

"A personal thing."

"Was it more surgery?"

"No."

"Drugs?"

"No!"

"Another man?"

"I would tell you if it was a man."

She had a point. Angela always shared the sordid details of her affairs.

"I cannot tell you. It is too shameful. If it got out, they would run me off the island."

"Who would?"

"Everyone."

"Angela."

Her gaze bounced back to me. "What?"

"Do I ever share your secrets with other people?"

"No. But they'll know."

"Is it worse than being a murder suspect? Because as soon as the police find out you own Wundebar Bread and hear you were on Skiathos yesterday, they'll put you on the list. Probably at the top."

She took a moment to think about it, head tilting left and

right. "Okay, I will tell you. I went to Skiathos to meet with Harry."

Well, well, well, I hadn't anticipated that. "Harry Vasilikos? Why? Were you lovers?"

"Never!"

"Kyria Sofia said you and Kyrios Harry were friends."

"Friends, no. He and my first husband did business sometimes, that is all. But he did have a sweet dog. Very obedient."

My eye twitched. "So why the clandestine meeting?"

"I want to open a supermarket and I want to stock his bread."

"You want to open a supermarket and stock Royal Pain bread?" I asked, incredulous. "Why?"

"Because I like it." She rose, smoothed her slacks. "Come with me."

I followed her through the light, spacious hallways with their pale art, until we reached a kitchen outfitted with brushed steel appliances and white marble counters. Everything was so clean that the five-second rule expanded to ten in this space. Angela opened one of several doors. A light came on inside a pantry bigger than my whole kitchen. One entire shelf was filled with bread—Royal Pain bread. I picked up a loaf to check the ingredients. Preservatives out the wazoo. This bread would stay fresh until the dinosaurs got a second shot at survival.

"Royal Pain is my favorite bread," Angela explained. "I cannot get enough of it."

"But Royal Pain your competitor."

"I didn't know that until today. I just like it."

"So you get it brought over from the mainland?"

"Most of the time. Sometimes I get it when I am there. This I got from Harry himself."

I froze. My throat dried up. "You got all this from Harry, yesterday?"

She shrugged. "Yes. I went to Skiathos to collect it because I did not want anyone here to see it being delivered when he arrived. You know how people on Merope are. Money or no money, that priest's sister would skewer me socially."

"Have you eaten any of it yet?"

"I still have an older loaf in the breadbox. Why?"

I grabbed my phone and called Leo. He answered on the second ring. When I told him to get his *kolos* over to Angela's house right away because the murder weapon in the Vasilikos case was potentially in her house, he sighed.

"I can pick it up but I can't do anything with it," he said.

The bottom fell out of my stomach. "Why not?"

"Because it's not my case anymore."

CHAPTER NINE

"Say it again for the slow person in the room," I said. "That's me."

"Harry Vasilikos and his passengers were dead several hours before they crashed. That means it's not our jurisdiction. Skiathos is part of the Thessaly region. Their police will be investigating now. Merope is the North Aegean region."

"So you're just giving up?"

"It's not our jurisdiction."

"So you're giving up." This time it wasn't a question.

He sighed. Looked to me like I wasn't the only frustrated one around here. "I'll be there in a few minutes."

A few turned out to be ten. While we were waiting, Angela's butler and I loaded up and carried the loaves to the foyer. Her butler is a British import because Greek butlers don't buttle authentically enough, I guess. Alfred is tall, thin, and if he has a sense of humor he keeps it in his back pocket next to a hip flask. Dealing with Angela twenty-four hours a day isn't for the sober or the sane.

Angela cast a mournful look at her lost carbs. "Why would anyone poison all this beautiful bread?"

"That's for the police to find out. Not our police, unfortunately, but police."

She air-kissed my cheeks. "You saved my life. If I had eaten that bread I would be dead." She thought about that a moment. "But then every man who had ever wronged me would be sorry, and maybe they would have cried at my funeral."

"Angela?"

"What?"

"Open that supermarket and take a break from men."

———

Leo filled his trunk with bread.

"Did ghosts tell you the bread was poisoned, or was it your superior research skills?"

"Yes."

"Which one?"

I passed him another armful of loaves. "I'm amazing at research."

"Are you going to tell me why you vanished on our date?"

"No."

One of these days maybe I would, when I had backup and pictures of the dead women. I needed to sit down and peruse missing persons' records, victims of solved and unsolved murders, until I had names to go with the faces. Right now I didn't have the stomach for all that death. At the moment I was consumed by the Vasilikos case. Leo could give up—had to give up—but I couldn't. Harry Vasilikos had something I wanted so badly I could taste it. There was a time when Andreas was my world. Then ... he was gone. Before Andreas left, I'd never been abandoned. Like any heart of a certain age, mine already had cracks before we fell in love, but when he left my heart shattered.

I needed to know where he was now.

If he was okay.

If any part of him still loved me.

If he was *sorry*.

"Do you want to try again? Lunch. Drinks. Coffee at Merope's Best. I know—what about a movie at my place? We could order dinner from Crusty Dimitri's. We could get food poisoning together."

Our heads turned simultaneously. We looked down at the bread.

"Bad joke," he said.

I tossed him the last three loaves, ticking them off like fingers. "It's a good joke. The timing was bad, that's all. And I don't want to try again."

"Is it because of Toula?"

The last loaf was in his trunk.

"No. It's because of me."

———

The day caught up to me. When it did, it slapped me until I was sleepy. All the way home I yawned. When I got there, Dead Cat was at the door, waiting. He wasn't always around but come nighttime he appeared and kept me company. When I wasn't in bed, he was on the couch, watching and waiting for me to leave my desk. Sometimes, like the other afternoon on the cliff, he showed up while I was working.

Of course, lately he wasn't my only ghost. Harry and his womenfolk were there, waiting. The women wanted me to change the channel, and Harry wanted to know when I was going to solve his murder.

"You gave Angela Zouboulaki bread," I said, shrugging off my coat. It went on the coatrack next to the door.

He shrugged. "Is that a crime? She loves my bread."

"Your poisoned bread."

"I didn't know that when I gave it to her."

I dumped my things on the desk, plugged my phone into the charger. "You could have told me you gave her the bread."

"My memory is not what it used to be. These days I do not have a brain."

He had a point and it was a good one—or would have been if I trusted the man.

"Want to know what I think?"

Kyrios Harry made a face. "No."

"Then it's your lucky night because I'm going to tell you anyway." My finger poked a hole in the air. "I think you are holding out on me." That same finger swung around to point at *Kyria* Eva. "And you ..."

"What about my sister?" Harry demanded.

"Somebody could have told me she's married to Johnny Margas. In fact, she owns the boat he sailed in on today."

Kyrios Harry's face turned red. "What?" He swung around to shoot eye daggers at his sister. "Is this true? For how long?"

Interesting. Very interesting. "You didn't know?" I asked *Kyrios* Harry.

"Of course I did not know. You think I would let my sister marry that *malakas*?

"Two years," *Kyria* Eva said. "We have been married for two wonderful years. And do you know why they have been wonderful? Because you did not know."

"Divorce him!"

"No." *Kyria* Eva pulled herself into a tall, fragile column and stuck her chin out. "What are you going to do? Kill me?" She stuck her chin out further. "I would like to see you *try*."

I went to the kitchen for water. "I just want to remind you that you're currently in critical condition in a hospital bed and that you could go at any time."

The bikini babes were lined up against the back of my couch, fixated on the family feud.

"I wish we could still eat popcorn," one said.

"If you're married to Johnny Margas, what were you doing on the Royal Pain?" I asked her. "And how did you keep your marriage secret all this time?"

"When you are rich is it easier to hide things," *Kyria* Eva said.

Her brother nodded. "Things like money, yes, but people?"

Kyria Eva stuck her finger in his face. "What do you know about anything? All you know is bread. People hide secret babies, marriages, addictions, all kinds of things."

"To be fair, it's a lot harder to hide things in Greece than most places," I said.

"Except money," Kyrios Harry said. "Greeks can hide money better than anyone. We hid all of ours and now we are using Germany's money."

Over-simplified, but sort-of correct.

My phone rang.

"I want you to stay away from the Vasilikos case," Leo said before I could say anything.

"Why?"

"Because someone murdered those people. Remember last time you got involved in a homicide? You could have been killed."

As if I could forget. Kyria Olga was my best friend.

"So you want me to drop it because you're worried about my safety?"

"Yes. I care about you."

In the one corner, Excitement was lacing its gloves. In the other, Terror was getting a pep talk from Survival Instinct. The fight happened fast. Terror knocked Excitement on its tailbone.

"It's not your place to worry about me, Detective Samaras. I'm thirty-one-years-old and I didn't stay alive this long by being stupid."

"I'm not saying you're stupid. I know you're not." He lowered his voice. "Look, whoever did this, they're not some old woman. This was somebody with resources and access to a wealthy man's property. You think it was easy to kill them? This took somebody with skill, and if you snoop around, you might be next."

"They were killed on their way *to* Merope—not *on* Merope. If the killer was here then wouldn't they wait until Harry Vasilikos and his friends reached the island?"

"You don't know that."

"Neither do you. It's been a couple of days and no one knows much of anything yet."

He sighed. "Allie, the Thessaly Police won't be happy if you stomp on their turf. We're more casual here."

"I'll keep that in mind."

"Why do you care about this case so much, can you at least tell me that?"

"It's personal."

"Did you know someone on that yacht?"

"No."

He went quite for a moment. Finally, he said, "Is it something to do with Andreas?"

I froze. "Don't say his name. You didn't know him."

"I did, actually. I grew up here, remember? Yes, I was away for a long time, but I knew Andreas. I liked him a lot. We weren't close but I considered him a friend. When he—"

"Don't."

"Okay." A long, heavy silence happened. My least favorite kind. "Just do me a favor and stay away from the Vasilikos case. I know you don't want me to care, but I do. Give me one less thing to worry about."

Without another word, I ended the call. The tug-of-war in my head continued. A gooey, melty feeling on one team, fear of winding up in a casket on the other. Unlike real life tug-of-war, all this emotional tugging with no win for either team in sight made me cranky. PMS times a hundred. And did I have chocolate? No. No, I did not. This was not a happy thing.

Leo. Andreas. Leo. Andreas.

Why didn't I have any sugar in this place? And why were these *malakes* still arguing in *my* apartment?

"And I wish you'd all leave," I snapped, "but I don't see me getting that anytime soon either."

The siblings quit bickering.

"Why not?" *Kyrios* Harry asked. "I promised I would leave when you solved my murder."

"Because your murder, and theirs" I waved at the women "is out of the local police's jurisdiction."

He shrugged. "So? You are not the police."

"I've done all I can do. I discovered the potential murder weapon and I've taken notes of all my conversations with the suspects I have access to, which is basically none. In the morning, I'm turning everything over to the Thessaly Police. And if you won't tell me what happened to Andreas, fine. Tonight, I'm too tired to care."

On that note, I slammed my bedroom door, threw myself down on the bed.

Lights out.

———

I wanted to say it was a natural waking, but there's nothing natural about being woken up at the crack of dawn by a rooster. Chicken enthusiasts can kiss my *kolos*.

Okay, I liked chickens—mmm ... chicken wings—but not

roosters. And I didn't like waking up before the sun had booted the moon out of the sky.

I rolled over and came face to face with Dead Cat. He was hunched on my extra pillow, overbite pointed in my direction, watching me come to terms with this whole waking up early thing.

"You need a name. A real name. I can't keep calling you Dead Cat. That's not a name, it's a description. Ginger? No. Also a description. Let me work on it."

The dead cat revved his motor.

Outside, the rooster crowed again. As dangerously as it was living, that bird was destined to become a sandwich filling.

Dead Cat remained on my pillow while I went to grab my laptop and phone. Normally I don't mix business and pleasure —and sleeping was definitely pleasure—but my living room was still crowded with the dead and the half-dead. Back against the headboard, covers yanked up to my chest, I opened my laptop and checked my email. A few new jobs had popped into my inbox overnight. Most were small and I cleared them off my to-do list quickly. My voicemail contained more paying work. One job I'd have to take care of in person. Missing jewelry. Not a theft, therefore not a police matter. So they'd called me, and could I please come to the family farm this morning?

Oooh, email from Jimmy Kontos. How exciting. What did the little twerp want this time?

I clicked on his email.

Help me get a date with Lydia.

Great. Now he wanted me to be a pimp.

Not a pimp, I told him.

His reply shot right back.

Please?

Still not a pimp.

But I really like her.
But I'm really not a pimp.
You stink, even for a giant.
And you're short, even for a nanos.

I closed the laptop and pulled the covers over my head. If Jimmy wanted a date with Lydia he needed to do it the old fashioned way, like the rest of us: by potentially humiliating himself. Finders Keepers wasn't a dating service. People's love lives were their own business.

Fists rained on my front door.

What now?

I stomped out and peered through the peephole. Nobody was there, that's how I knew Jimmy Kontos was on the other side. I yanked open the door.

"What?"

No answer. He pushed past me and planted his *kolos* on my couch. His legs dangled. His feet didn't have a hope of touching the floor. He was wearing jeans with too much cuff and boots with too much heel.

What was worse: the uninvited ghosts or the uninvited shrimp?

"Are those high heels?"

"What? No."

"Because those look like high heels to me. Maybe we need a second opinion. If only I knew someone who lives and breathes fashion. Someone who lives across the hall."

His eyes narrowed. "Don't you dare." He wiggled his butt down into my couch cushions and dropped his boots on my coffee table.

"Did you miss the part where I didn't invite you in?"

Jimmy checked me out. He made a face—at least I think he did. It was hard to tell under all that hair. "Is that what you sleep in? No wonder you're single."

I held the door open. "Get out."

"No wonder you have no friends," Harry Vasilikos said from his spot by the window. He sure enjoyed that view of the parking lot.

"I have friends," I snapped.

Jimmy's head swiveled. "Are you crazy? Because that would make a lot of sense. You seem like a crazy person."

This was hell, and I was in it.

"What do you want, Jimmy? You want me to get you a date with Lydia? I'll call her right now and ask her."

He jumped up. "Not so loud. She might hear you."

"Isn't that the point? That's how you get a date: by using words."

"Boy, for a smart person you sure are a *vlakas*."

"I like this *nanos*," Harry said. I shot him with my best stink-eye.

"If you want help, drop the insults." I aimed my words at both of them.

Jimmy held up both his hands in supplication, not the open-palmed *moutsa*. "Okay, okay. I'll be good."

Slowly, I closed the door. I wasn't ready to sit yet, so I folded my arms and leaned against the door as a reminder that I could easily pick him up and toss him out.

"Talk," I said. "But not too much."

Jimmy mimed writing with a pen. "I want you to write her a love letter for me."

"Are you illiterate? I know some good teachers."

"No, I can read and write you giant—"

Dirty look. Filthy. And not in a good way.

"—did I mention you are amazing? And you look good in whatever that is you are wearing, even if it is old pajamas? That's old pajamas, yes?"

"Hmm ..."

He flopped back against my cushions, head in hands. "I can write but I can't write love letters."

"And you think I can?"

"Of course. You're a woman."

"Well, this woman can't write love letters." That was a lie. I could and I had. Ask whoever handled the Backstreet Boys' fan mail. I could write love letters with the worst of them.

"Okay," he said. "Can you order flowers?"

"That I can do, but why can't you do it yourself?"

"I want it to be anonymous. Nobody on this island can keep a secret."

Good point. If he ordered flowers on Merope, even anonymously, the moment Lydia called them to ask about her secret admirer, the island's only florist would spit out Jimmy's name.

"All right, I'll order flowers for her. But that's as far as I go. I meant it when I said I'm not a pimp."

Jimmy rubbed his hands together. He wiggled off the couch and pulled out his wallet. "Go get dressed."

"Now? It's barely light out. The florist won't open until nine."

"If you go now you'll be first in line. I really like this woman."

I sighed and took his money, which included enough for an extravagant bouquet of flowers and more than enough to cover my time and trouble. Jimmy was a *malakas* but he wasn't cheap.

"Any preferences?"

"Roses," he said. "Women always love roses."

———

Kyria Hondrou's family farm had been churning out chickens since my family starting eating them, generations ago. Hondrou chickens swung from meathooks in the windows of Merope's meat shops (never call it a butcher's shop, otherwise they'll think you're shopping for penis), with and without feathers. The birds were always plump and delicious, thanks to a secret ingredient Kyria Hondrou mixed with their feed. The secret ingredient was ouzo, or so my secret source told me. Hondrou birds died as they had lived: relaxed and happy.

Kyria Hondrou was from my grandmother's generation. Kyria Hondrou's figure resembled the birds she raised: scrawny knock-knees, over-developed breasts that hung at waist-level. Her chicken figure was was shrouded in black. She propped up her stoop with a cane. Her eyes were black marbles, pressed into puckered holes. They saw everything and they didn't like any of it. She had one eyebrow that ran from temple to temple, a wide thick strip with gnarled hairs of varying lengths. The monobrow was terrifying and I couldn't quit looking at it. No one could. It was like someone had hammered a weasel to death with a mallet and stapled it to her face. Tourists who encountered Kyria Hondrou's monobrow raced to the store for tweezers and wax. She was the reason threading was a thing on Merope.

This was my first visit to the Hondrou family farm. Kyria Hondrou was sitting in a green-and-white striped deck chair that was more rust than metal. Through beady eyes, she watched scores of chickens peck at the ground. She didn't greet me. That duty fell on the shoulders of her daughter-in-law, Eleni, who spent her days running around after the chickens like they were an extra set of children. Eleni did everything, and she never did it well enough. Eleni and her husband had five children, none of whom made Kyria Hondrou happy.

According to Eleni, a thin, quiet woman who I'd gone to high school with, Kyria Hondrou had managed to lose the crucifix that hung from her neck, despite the fact that she never left her chair, except to travel to the outhouse and back, and to and from her bed in the kitchen, twice each day.

"It is silver," Kyria Hondrou said, fixing those dark holes on my face. "Worth a fortune."

No point telling her that as far as metals go, silver wasn't worth much these days.

"What does it look like?" I asked.

Kyria Hondrou snorted like a bull. "You do not go to church? It is a crucifix. It looks like this." Arms up and out. Chin on chest. The monobrow stared at me. I couldn't look away.

"Silver, you said?"

"Silver." She thumped her cane on the packed dirt. "I will sit here and watch while you look for it."

I swung around and looked at Eleni. "Where was it lost?"

"Here on the farm," Kyria Hondrou barked.

Eleni shrugged. "Somewhere in the yard." She blinked. I wondered if it was Morse Code for "help me."

Big yard. Lots of places to lose a necklace. Chickens everywhere. Long, low troughs filled with Kyria Hondrou's magical fowl food. Dilapidated sheds. A tree stump, the top criss-crossed with axe wounds. Maroon stains. A gleaming axe leaning against the stump.

Meat comes from a supermarket, I reminded myself. It doesn't swing from hooks after losing its head on a tree stump.

"Do not think you will get a free chicken," Kyria Hondrou said, following my gaze.

"I don't eat chicken," I lied.

"Everybody eats chicken," she said.

"Vegetarians don't eat chicken, Mama," Eleni said.

"Who asked you?"

I circled the yard. Chill chickens followed me.

"Where are you going?" Kyria Hondrou tapped her cane on the ground. "*Vre*, Eleni, where is she going?"

"I'm looking for your necklace," I said.

Eleni excused herself. She had to fix lunch for the family and get away from her mother-in-law, probably before she was temped to use that axe. I was casting the sharp blade longing gazes, too.

Kyria Hondrou raised her cane, used to it point to the far corner of the yard, where someone had set up a paddling pool for Eleni's kids. "There."

"In the pool?"

"In the pool."

"And you couldn't reach in and get it yourself?"

Her monobrow dipped in the center. "That is what you do, no?"

I suppressed a groan. Taking her money when all I had to do was bend down and pluck the necklace out of the water was robbery.

The monobrow was watching me. "How much?"

"Don't worry about it," I said. "I can't charge you for this."

For the first time in human history, she smiled. "This is what I hoped you would say."

I rolled up my sleeves and trotted over to the paddling pool.

And recoiled.

It was a paddling pool, yes, but something was seriously wrong with the contents. If it was water it had been filtered through a chicken's digestive system. The pool was filled to the brim with greenish-brown paste that glistened ominously in the sun.

The stench of chicken *kaka* punched me in the stomach. I gagged.

Kyria Hondrou hit the ground with her cane. "What are you waiting for, eh?"

"This is full of chicken *kaka*."

"Good news, you are not blind."

I stared at the pool. Where was the Vicks Vapor Rub when I needed it?

"Hurry up," she said.

Virgin Mary, she expected me to stick my hand in there for a cheap necklace? "Do you have any rubber gloves? A hazmat suit?"

"No." Her eyes gleamed. "No gloves."

I swung around and looked at the pool again. What kind of freak hoarded chicken crap?

"Is there a reason you're collecting this?"

"Yes."

I waited. She didn't elaborate.

Oh boy. For this I needed rubber gloves. No way could I stick my bare hand in there, not even for Christ on his cross. I rolled down my sleeve.

"I'll be back with tweezers," I said.

"What?"

"Gloves. I meant rubber gloves. I have to go but I'll be back soon with rubber gloves."

She rose out of her chair and hobbled over, one hand supporting her lower back. The chickens followed her. They knew she was feeding their addiction, enhancing their calm.

"For what? You will not be able to find my necklace with big rubber gloves on your hands. Maybe that is what you want. Or maybe you want to hide my necklace in your glove and keep it for yourself. What kind of person steals from an old woman, eh? What would your *yiayia* say if she knew you were a thief?"

Knowing Yiayia, she wouldn't have said a word. Instead, she would have grabbed Kyria Hondrou by the messy bun and shoved her into the pool, face first. Or maybe that was wishful thinking on my part.

Slowly, reluctantly, like a peasant on the way to the gallows, I shucked my jacket, rolled up my sleeve to the elbow.

"Higher. I want to make sure you do not steal from me." Her gnarled, olive twig of a finger wagged in my face. "And remember, you promised to do this for free."

———

It took me thirty minutes to dredge the bottom of the paddling pool with my bare fingers. I recovered one dead rat, three pebbles, and something I think used to be reading glasses. No sign of Kyria Hondrou's chain and crucifix—or my dignity.

I looked at my manure-covered arm. There was a good chance it was unsalvageable. Probably they'd have to amputate.

"Why you stop?" she barked.

"It's not in here."

The old woman shrugged. "Maybe it is somewhere else."

"Somewhere else," I said flatly.

"Wait." She reached into her apron pocket. Out came her withered hand, a silver chain coiled around her fingers. "I found it. You can leave now."

I sat back on my haunches, the scream trapped in my throat.

What are you waiting for?" she said.

"I spent thirty minutes sifting through chicken *kaka*."

"So?"

I looked at her. Hard.

"You get nothing," she said, jabbing her cane at me. "I did your job for you."

———

I peddled toward home with my sleeve rolled up and my coat scrunched in my bicycle's basket. The stink of chicken manure wafted up my nose. Eleni had kindly let me rinse off under the yard's pump, but frigid water doesn't do squat for poop. For that you need soap. A lot of soap. And possibly bleach.

As I approached the More Super Market, I spotted the Triantafillou brothers sitting outside in a pair of dilapidated chairs. Yiorgos and Dimitri, the Triantafillou brothers, were a pair of potatoes, baked too long in a slow oven. Their skins were too loose for their bodies. They wore their pants hoisted almost to their armpits. Each man came with a walking stick and a thick wallet. My *yiayia* used to say the brothers could squeeze money from a corpse, even if no one had been using the corpse as a place to hide their savings. Neither brother was married; Yiayia also said they planned to live forever or take it all to the grave. Looking at them, I was glad they had a Plan B.

These same Triantafillou brothers had a meeting scheduled with Harry Vasilikos, before the bread baron perished between islands. Which meant I wanted to talk to them, Thessaly Police or no Thessaly Police.

I rolled to a stop, wished them a *kalimera*—good morning —even though I'd spent the morning elbow-deep in chicken waste and therefore there wasn't much good about this particular morning, except that eventually it would be over.

The men wrinkled the root vegetables they called noses. Their eyes watered. "What is that smell?" Kyrios Dimitri asked.

"Chicken manure," I told him.

"Ah. You have been to see *Kyria* Hondrou. That woman is sour, like the lemon."

"And that thing on her face," *Kyrios* Yiorgos said. "What is that? A dead animal? Who can say?"

There was a shower not too far away and it was calling my name.

"Did you hear about Harry Vasilikos?" I asked them.

"We heard," *Kyrios* Yiorgos said.

"Someone mentioned you were supposed to have a business meeting with him about distributing Royal Pain bread."

"Sure. A meeting," Kyrios Yiorgos said. "But then Harry went and crashed into the island, and now there is no meeting."

"Did you know him well?"

"He used to spend summers here, but not for a long time. We have not seen him in five years."

"More like twenty," *Kyrios* Dimitri said.

"Twenty? How can it be twenty when he was here five years ago."

"Twenty," his brother repeated.

"Five."

"*Re malaka*, it was twenty years. Maybe longer."

The conversation devolved quickly. While the brothers bickered, I wished them a good morning and rode away. I'd get back to them later, when I wasn't covered in chicken manure.

———

One long, hot shower later—heavy on the soap and shampoo —I was almost fit for human consumption again. Almost. The smell was still there, lingering in my mucus membranes. I shuddered as my brain dredged up the memory of me with my arm in the poop pool, complete with the sensation of chicken manure slick and slimy against my skin. Every time I moved, I caught a whiff of ammonia. Moving wasn't convenient right now for a couple of reasons, including the stink.

It was noon and the delivery boy had just thrust an obscenely huge bunch of roses at Olga Marouli's granddaughter. I knew this because I was peeping through my spy hole.

"Who are they from?" Lydia asked him.

The delivery boy shrugged. "A secret admirer, I think."

"I don't even like roses," she said.

"What is she doing?" Jimmy asked over the phone. It was pressed to my ear and I was trying to spy and communicate at the same time. Not easy when there was only a thin slab of wood standing between me and discovery.

"Wrinkling her nose," I whispered.

"In a good way or a bad way?"

"I don't think there is a good way."

"She doesn't like the roses?" He sounded crestfallen. "I thought all women liked roses."

"We're not a monolith, you know. We come in different colors, shapes, and sizes, just like underwear."

He ignored that. "What is she doing now? Is she reading the note?"

I squinted through the spy hole. Sure enough, Lydia was reading the card. The delivery boy, a local teenager who had dropped out of school to follow his dreams of being a delivery boy, went to leave. Lydia grabbed his shirt collar, yanked him back.

"Wait." She held up the card. "Who sent these?"

The kid shrugged. "I don't know. I just deliver flowers."

"How can I find out?"

"Ask *Despinidia* Diktaki? She owns the store."

Despinidia—Miss—Diktaki had inherited the florist from a rich, dead relative who wasn't dead or a relative. In fact, her very rich not-a-relative had a wife and seven children in a swanky Athens neighborhood. Nobody talked about the wife or the children—at least not to the florist's face.

"Where can I find her?"

He shrugged again. He did that a lot. Like most teenagers he didn't know much, even though he thought he knew it all. I had been there myself; I knew. At sixteen I was the smartest person on the planet and everyone else was an idiot.

"At the store?" he said. "She arranges all the flowers herself."

Lydia struck him with her smile. "Thanks." She shut the door, taking the flowers she didn't like with her.

The delivery boy adjusted the front of his pants, then he slunk off down the hall.

"She read the card," I told Jimmy. "Now she's gone to call the florist."

"So what do I do now?"

"Pray," I said.

"Pray for what?"

"That on some level, I have respect for you."

"Do you?"

"We're about to find out."

Apartment 201's door flew open. Lydia padded across the hall in fluffy slippers.

"Uh oh," I said. "Here we go."

"What?" Jimmy sounded worried.

"Wait."

Lydia knocked. "Allie, are you there? I need to talk to you."

There was no point delaying the inevitable. I took a deep breath. I opened the door.

"No," I said.

"I still don't know if I like you," she said, "but you're funny, so it's looking good. Did you send me flowers?"

"On behalf of a client, yes."

Her eyes lit up. "Who?"

"I can't tell you." What do you know, I did have some

respect for Jimmy Kontos after all. Not much, but it was better than nothing.

"Man or woman?"

"Man."

She twiddled a hank of her hair and chewed on the ends. "Is it someone I know?"

"Give me a list of everyone you know and I'll tell you."

She laughed. "Okay, let me think."

I waited.

"Do you smell something?" she said.

"No. And it's especially not chicken manure."

Her cute nose wrinkled. "A work thing?"

"Indentured servitude or maybe an act of reluctant charity. Either way, I didn't get paid."

"You should go back and demand hazard pay." She looked back at her apartment. "The roses. Was it Johnny Margas? I bet it was. I heard he's here on the island."

My mouth wanted to fall open but my brain kept it shut. "You know Johnny Margas?"

"We've met." She winked at me. Obviously we had very different definitions of the word.

"Did you know he's married?"

"Lots of rich men are married. That doesn't stop them sending flowers to young, attractive women."

Behind me, *Kyria* Eva gasped.

Lydia couldn't hear her. She carried on speculating. "They are from Johnny, aren't they? It would be just like him to send something old fashioned like roses without stopping to consider what I like. Women are widgets to men like him. Our *mounis* are interchangeable. The same hole with different faces."

I thought about *Kyria* Eva and Angela, both betrayed by Johnny Margas. If he kept it up, he would wind up a dead man.

"It wasn't Johnny Margas," I said. "The roses are from a much better class of man. And if or when I get permission to give you his name, I will."

"Aww, I'm touched," Jimmy said in my ear.

A sly look crept over Lydia's pretty face. "What if I hire you to find out who sent me the flowers?"

I laughed. "I don't know if I like you either, but you're funny, too."

Shrug. "It was worth a try."

She went back to her apartment, leaving me with a wailing *Kyria* Eva, six ghosts, and a cheering Jimmy Kontos.

"You're good," Jimmy said over the phone. "So good I could kiss you. Too bad you're a giant. So what do we do next?"

"What you do is relax. You've already piqued her curiosity."

I could hear him rubbing his hands together. At least, I hoped it was his hands.

"Thanks," he said. "I owe you."

I reminded him that he'd already paid me in money, then I ended the call. Now I had to deal with these ghosts and the weeping Kyria Eva.

My hands found my hips. I put on my best stern, non-sexy librarian face.

"If you were solid, I'd pour you a glass of ouzo. But you aren't really here, so sit up, shut up, and listen."

"You can't talk to me like that," *Kyria* Eva said, sniveling.

"She is talking to you like that, and you deserve it," *Kyrios* Harry said. "Sit."

Kyria Eva's bottom hit my office chair.

"Johnny Margas is *kaka*," I said. "He's a cheating, no-good, murder suspect. And when you wake up and get out of that hospital bed, you need to get a good lawyer and leave him."

"I can't do that," she wailed.

"Why not?"

With a twist of an internal faucet, the crying stopped. She wiped her hand across her eyes.

"Because he is in my hospital room right now, and I think he is going to kill me."

CHAPTER TEN

I couldn't dial Leo's number fast enough.

"Where are you?" I yelled into the phone.

Groggy voice. Slurring words. "In bed. Why?"

"Johnny Margas is going to kill his wife."

"Who?" His tone sharpened—fast.

"Johnny Margas. Real name: Yiannis Margas."

Upstairs, his feet hit the floor. "And who is his wife?"

"Eva Vasiliko." Virgin Mary, he had no idea who I was talking about because they hadn't identified her yet. "She's your survivor, the one you're supposed to be guarding."

"We are guarding her, at least until the Thessaly Police move her."

"There won't be anyone to move if you don't get Margas away from her right now."

He ended the call.

"*Skata na fas*," I muttered. The dead women giggled because I had just told Detective Samaras to eat poop. More precisely, I'd said "Shit to eat." The Greek language doesn't string words together the same way English does. I called the hospital, told them to get up to the ICU right now to check on the crash's lone survivor.

Someone knocked on the door. I yanked it open to find Leo there in sweat pants and a t-shirt with a leather jacket thrown over the top.

"Come on," he said.

"Where are we going?"

"The hospital. And you are coming with me because I have questions."

"You didn't call the police—I mean Merope's other police?"

"Relax, I called them. But I still have to go."

I grabbed my bag, shoved my feet into boots and followed him downstairs. Hopefully he wasn't taking me somewhere to cut off my head.

He opened the car door for me. I flinched as he reached over and buckled me in.

"Why do you do that?"

"I like touching you," he said. "Why do you look like I'm going to take you somewhere to cut off your head?"

Yikes. Was he a mind reader? I looked in the passenger mirror. No. I really did look like I was on my way to my own beheading.

"I spent the morning digging through a paddling pool filled with chicken manure."

"Work or pleasure?"

Under the circumstances, I couldn't laugh. But I wanted to.

"Neither. I got conned by an old woman."

Thirty seconds later we were speeding along the streets of Merope, toward the hospital.

"Pappas is at the hospital. He's the one I called," Leo said.

"Did he stop Margas?"

"I don't know yet." He glanced me. "How do you know the survivor's name?"

"I can't tell you."

"If you tell me, I can keep it confidential."

"Okay. She told me herself."

He flashed another look at me, this one disbelieving. "How is that possible?"

"I don't know. I'm trying to figure that out myself. Ghosts I'm used to, but people in comas? This is a first."

The car slowed. Distracted by my revelation, Leo had pulled his foot off the gas.

"Ghosts. People in comas," he muttered.

"Keep driving," I said.

He jammed his foot down. The car shot forward.

"Ghosts," he said again, dazed.

"Yes."

"That's crazy."

"The world is a crazy place. You really have no idea how crazy. I'm not sure I even know how crazy it is, which kind of bothers me. If ghosts exist, then why not other things?"

I had contemplated the possibility before, just not out loud and in front of other people.

"So Harry Vasilikos and his sister. Who were the other victims?"

"I don't know their names. They're Harry Vasilikos's companions."

"Companions?"

"People who keep other people company."

Leo clammed up. Not a word out of him the rest of the way to the hospital, which wasn't far. When Leo parked I had to open my own door. He was already loping ahead, leaving me in the dust. Well, he had wanted the truth, hadn't he? The detective had left me no choice. There was no way to lie about my source; my details were too detailed. And now he couldn't handle that truth. Colonel Jessup was right.

I hurried after Leo. He took the stairs two at a time.

On the second floor I caught up to him. He cut into the cluster of cops around what I guessed was Eva Vasiliko's door. Johnny Margas was there, too, hands splayed, mouth working fast, spitting out words. He didn't do anything, he was saying. He was adjusting his wife's pillows, that's all.

"Adjusting them all over her face?" Constable Pappas asked. "Because that's what you were doing."

Hands in his pants pockets, Johnny Margas shrugged. "She always sleeps with a pillow over her head."

"Really?" Leo said. Cop face on. Hard and cool. Magnetic and simultaneously repelling. I kind of wanted him to use his handcuffs on me. My Virgin Mary, why did he have to be a whacko killer?

Johnny Margas opened his mouth, presumably to proclaim his innocence again, then he spotted me standing there, trying to blend in with the paint and a rack of bedpans. "You again."

Leo glanced at me. "You've met?"

"He was trying to get into a client's *sovraka*." I didn't mention Angela's name or what kind of underwear she wore. "Can I see her?" My question was directed at Leo.

A long moment passed, then he nodded once. "For a second."

I slipped into Kyria Eva's hospital room. The bone-thin woman was unrecognizable. Lots of bandages. Her bare skin was scorched and crispy. She looked like a half-baked turkey. Her eyes were open.

"Allie," she rasped.

Eva Vasiliko was awake.

———

One audible gasp later—mine—Leo was ejecting me from the ICU.

"You can't be here," he said. "She is either a victim or a suspect, and it is up to the Thessaly Police to decide which. They will go crazy if they know you've been in to see her."

"What about Johnny Margas?"

Pappas was already marching Johnny Margas down the hallway, hands cuffed. The older man had lost his swagger and the color in his skin. Maybe he liked handcuffs but not like this.

"If he tried to kill his wife, this is our jurisdiction, not Thessaly's" His eyes softened. "Go home. We'll talk later. I'll make sure *Kyria* Vasilikos is okay." He put his keys in my hand and closed my fingers around them. They were warm and strong—his fingers, not his keys. "Take my car."

"What about you?"

"I will call you if I need a ride home."

———

Leo's car wouldn't fit in the street outside the Cake Emporium. It was a space designed for donkeys, bicycles, and a maximum of two gossiping widows walking abreast. So I parked in the main street and hoofed it to what had become my favorite confectionary store. I couldn't go another night without more sugar. Not if was anything like last night.

Betty hugged me. She was warm and tiny, and she felt like home and smelled like marshmallows and cream.

"Perfect timing, as always, luv. I just whipped up a couple of treats for us."

The treats turned out to be a pair of caramel hot chocolates, served with tiny marshmallows and chocolate freckles on the side. Stress slid out of my body. Boneless, I flopped down on one of the small sofas and reached for the closest mug of heaven.

"My life is weird," I said, breathing in a curl of chocolate and caramel steam. "Too weird. I need more sugar in my life. Diabetes schmiabetes."

Her eyes twinkled. "Lucky for you then that I know a place you can get some. You can tell me what you'd like or you can leave it to me to pack a box filled with things I know you'll love. I'm good at figuring out what my customers like."

"That sounds perfect," I said. "I'll leave my gastronomical delights in your capable hands."

Betty beamed, hugged me around the shoulders. "Then while I'm doing that, you drink that hot chocolate and tell me what's on your mind."

"Murder and mayhem, mostly. One more murder and this will become the new normal. I don't want it to be the new normal. I like my quiet life where I find things for people."

Betty placed a large white cake box on the counter. Her head disappeared as she got busy picking and choosing from the big cabinets. Her voice wafted over the top. "To be alive is to change, I'm afraid. You can turn your back on change, but like a puppy, that change will keep sitting its bottom down in front of you, demanding you pay it attention."

"What if I ignore it?"

"The puppy?"

"Change."

"Eventually it will switch tactics, won't it? What was a cute puppy will become a giant hammer, and that hammer will *boop* you over the head until you yield and evolve."

"I was afraid of that." The hot drink was making me drowsy. "I've got a ghost in my apartment that isn't a ghost."

"Not all apparitions are ghosts," she said.

I looked up from the caramel hot chocolate. "What did you say?"

"You're projecting those words in neon. Whoever told you that had a good point. Not every woo-woo thing used to be alive. And some, like your *Kyria* Eva, are alive enough, but their bodies are damaged or sleeping."

"Are you saying vampires are real?"

"Every story, every myth, every rumor or legend starts somewhere with a seed of truth. Maybe vampires aren't bloodsucking fiends who hunt virgins at night, but maybe there was someone once who fancied a tipple of blood now and then."

"What about zombies?"

"Men and women enslaved by powerful medicines that hold them in a thrall."

"Werewolves?"

"Perhaps you should ask *Kyria* Sofia about werewolves. I hear she knows a thing or two about exotic animals."

I choked on the hot chocolate. Spluttered. "*Kyria* Sofia, Father Spiros's sister? You know about that?"

Her head popped up above the glass cabinet. A mischievous grin reached up from her lips to dance in her eyes. She winked.

"You are terrible," I said, laughing.

"Everybody has secrets, and thanks to my gift I see far too many of them. Now, Greece is interesting because it has all the usual woo-woo things, plus its own."

"Don't tell me the Olympians were real."

"Remember, there is truth in fiction. Every fantastical thing starts with that seed of truth, even those crackpots from Mount Olympus. Can you imagine what a philandering nightmare the real Zeus must have been?"

"You know a lot about this stuff."

"We all have our talents. You have a knack for finding things and convening with the dead, and I am a fount of knowledge when it comes to things that go, 'Knock, knock, can I borrow a cup of sugar?' in the middle of the night." She reappeared on my side of the cabinets with the cakebox. "Something sweet for every occasion," she said, presenting me with the box. "Too bad that big teddy bear of a cat can't share."

———

I shooed the dead women off my couch, flicked the television to something I liked, opened my box of cakes. The women peered into the box. They made happy sounds.

"I would kill someone to be able taste cake one more time," one of the women said. I don't know which one. They were interchangeable. Which was offensive now that I thought about it. They were individuals—or had been—and it was wrong of me to think of them as a monolith, just because they all wore the same hairstyle and visited the same plastic surgeon. Virgin Mary, I was no better than Jimmy Kontos or Johnny Margas.

"What are your names?" I asked them.

Maria, Maria, Maria, Maria, and Maria.

"You have issues," I told Harry. "Was your mother's name Maria?"

He shrugged it off. "Can I help it if they are all Maria? They were all Maria when they asked to come on my boat."

Kyria Eva was, predictably, gone. Six to go.

"Your sister is fine, by the way. Nice of you to ask." I went to the kitchen for a fork and spoon. It pays to be prepared.

Harry did not turn away from the window. "She is alive and I am dead."

On the television screen, Keanu Reeves spotted the white rabbit and prepared to go Alice by heading to the club to meet Trinity. I did the same thing, cracking open a white chocolate mummy with edge of a spoon. Raspberry cream oozed out, streaked with real raspberries.

Keanu was cute. He wasn't Leo Samaras but he made leather look good.

Leo. Was he killer or not?

Not all apparitions are ghosts.

What if the dead women from our date weren't dead or women? Like Fox Mulder, I wanted to believe.

Another confection later—a dark chocolate witch's hat filled with nuts and caramel—Keanu was taking another leap of faith. Maybe I needed to do the same thing. I had a head full of loose facts, flopping around like mismatched socks out of the dryer. Now that the Thessaly Police had seized the Royal Pain case, I had time to think about other things until the status quo stopped status quo-ing.

I carried my laptop to the couch, propped my feet up on the coffee table. Good thing my mother and sister were not here to witness that travesty.

The hunt was on. Objective: Find the two dead women who had muscled in on my date with Detective Leo Samaras.

What did I already know?

Leo hadn't been back on Merope for long. He was raised on the island, then he'd left for a long stretch before returning as the local police detective. His last known location on the mainland was Thessaloniki, the country's second largest city. Thessaloniki is a major hub for people and cargo traveling to and from southeastern Europe. A murder or ten could happen there and be swept under a rug or into the sea.

Or maybe there was no murder at all.

I started with homicides of women between the ages of eighteen and thirty five. In 2017 the country saw eighty-one murders, about a third of which were women. Within ten minutes I was looking at their faces—their unfamiliar faces. Leo was a couple of years older than me, so I went back twelve years, hunting for a face I recognized, hoping I wouldn't find one.

And I didn't.

Next: Missing persons, specifically women. There were hundreds of faces to sift through, women who were lost or worse. The second *Matrix* movie came and went and I had abandoned the cakes for the scores of women who had vanished.

Nothing.

Deaths were next. More interested in suicides, I narrowed my search and came up dry again. Same with deaths from natural causes and other assorted accidents.

Dry haul. I squished a piece of cake with the fork while I thought.

What if the women weren't Greek?

I picked up the phone and called Sam. Asked him to find out if Leo had left the country in the past twelve years. From the two apparitions' hairstyles and fashions I would guess they had been killed—if they were killed at all—within the past five years, but I was playing it safe by extending the search to twelve.

While I waited, I extended the searches by another decade.

No faces stood out.

Until one did.

CHAPTER ELEVEN

THE FALLING WOMAN from Merope's cliff smiled back at me. Maria Petsini was her name. Twenty-eight-years-old. Part of the fabric of the island for so long—at least as long as I'd been here—I had never paid her much attention before. She'd gone missing twenty years ago, somewhere between Athens and Thessaloniki.

At the time, her parents, Yiorgos and Maria Petsinis had offered a reward for information, the substantial sum of five thousand euros. (Given that Greece switched from the drachma to the euro fifteen years ago, the original sum would have been in drachmas.) The reward had never been claimed.

The poor Petsinis. Their daughter wasn't missing. She was long dead, her bones swept away to God only knew where.

Sam called back. "Your boy has never been anywhere. Doesn't even have a passport."

"Thanks, Sam."

He wasn't done. "Say, that cake shop of yours. Where did you tell me it was? I went rolling down the hill today to take a look. But maybe I'm getting old or something because I couldn't find the place."

I gave him directions again and ended the call. Sam was wrong about one thing. Just because Leo didn't have a passport, didn't mean he'd never left the country. All it meant was that he'd never visited a region outside the Schengen Area. That gave him twenty-six potential killing grounds.

I went back to Maria Petsini's face. Something about her was bothering me, but I couldn't put my finger on what that something was. Maybe it was me. Guilty feelings and all that. Next time I saw her I would try to be kinder. Maybe she would have information I could pass to her parents, so they could find some measure of peace—if there is such a thing for the parent of a dead child.

Frustrated, I flopped back onto the couch cushions. Ghost milled around me.

"Are you stressed? You look stressed," one of the Marias said. "What you need is a massage."

"I don't do massages."

"Massages are amazing," she said. "You should do massages."

"Too ticklish," I told her.

Another Maria had other ideas. "You should drink."

Now there was an idea I could get next to. In the kitchen cupboard there was an ouzo bottle with a solider on the label. The same bottle Toula had brought over after Kyria Olga's murder. Toula didn't always have a stick up her *kolos;* sometimes she could be downright human. I poured two fingers of ouzo and was this close to knocking it back when my phone rang.

"Come get me?"

Well, well, well, Detective Samaras.

"You just saved me from drinking and driving," I told him. "I was this close to ouzo oblivion."

"Bad night?"

"Let's just say my life took a weird turn recently and it isn't getting any less weird."

"The ghosts," he said dubiously.

"The ghosts have been around since forever. They're nothing new."

"What are you drinking?"

I told him and he chuckled. "Sounds like you need some food to soak up that ouzo."

He was right, drinking with food was the Greek way. It prevented a lot of blackouts and saved myriads from being outed as alcoholics. "What did you have in mind?"

"Pick me up and you'll find out."

I thought about the dead women from our date and the skeletons that didn't appear to be hiding in his closet—not yet, anyway. The possibility that he didn't kill those women raised questions. Questions with potentially complicated and terrible answers.

"No hints?"

"Food. That's the only hint you're getting."

Whatever it was, I hoped it didn't come with a side of murder.

———

"Are you joking?"

Leo slapped a white minty pill into my hand. "Take this."

"Why?"

"Preventative measure."

I handed it back. "Antacids won't save us from salmonella and E. coli."

"But it will stop us burping up Crusty Dimitri's gyros. Besides, we have ouzo, remember? Alcohol should kill the bacteria and parasites."

"I don't think there's any science in your science."

There was a knock on the door. It was the same kid who had delivered Lydia's flowers earlier today. He was really killing it as a delivery boy.

"I'm sorry," he said as he accepted Leo's money.

"Don't be," Leo told him. "Caveat emptor. What kind of meat is Dimitri serving tonight?"

"I don't know, but my neighbor's donkey went missing earlier this week."

I winced. There were only so many places a donkey could go on a small island. Crusty Dimitri's kitchen was one of them.

Leo took the bag and headed to my kitchen. The ghosts followed. Great. So we had an audience. Although, given that Leo might still be a serial killer, having ghosts around wasn't the worst idea ever. Maybe they could find some other poor sap to contact if this meal went wrong. At least one other person could see ghosts on the island. There was a chance I could yell *Kyrios* Stavros's name before I took my last breath.

Leo divvied up thick *tiganites*—fries—sprinkled with green flecks I hoped were oregano, and a couple of gyros that looked okay from a distance. Up close, the meat was oily and the *tzatziki* was more pungent than it should be, with something other than garlic.

"I don't think I can do this," I said. "If I eat it you'll have to transport me to Toula's house on my shield."

Leo carried the plates to my kitchen table. He poured water for two, and a glass of ouzo for himself. Mine was already on the table. For someone who didn't live here he was comfortable moving around in my space.

"That's what the ouzo is for," he said. "Courage. Where do you sit?"

I pointed to my seat. He took the other one.

He raised his glass. "Drink."

We drank. First one, then another. Two glasses later we were brave enough to tackle the food.

"I like this," he said.

My eyebrows rose. My mouth tried to open but I was busy holding back the vomit. I swallowed and instantly had regrets. "The food? How can you like the food?"

"I was talking about the company and the atmosphere. This is what we should have started with."

"It's too late for that now." Ouzo haze filled my head. My limbs were soft and floppy. For someone whose life was turning down dark corners, I felt good.

"Why did you run away?"

"Technically, I walked, then I climbed and shimmied, then I risked social suicide by slipping off my heels and hobbling home barefoot."

"Whatever you did, why did you do it?" He moved to pour more ouzo in my glass but I covered it with my hand.

I thought about all the dead and missing women I'd looked at today and now none were familiar except Maria Petsini, the perpetual cliff-jumper.

"I saw something."

"What?"

I pushed the plate away. I couldn't do this, not even with three glasses of ouzo in my stomach. "Women."

"Women?" He ditched the gyro and forked fried potato into his mouth. "At the taverna? I didn't see any women. All I saw was you running away."

"Walking."

"Walking away then." He ate another oregano-sprinkled potato. "Is this another ghost thing?"

"I don't know what it is."

And I didn't, because like last time, the woman stepped out of nowhere and into my kitchen. No shimmering air that normally occurred in the split second before a ghost appeared. She wasn't here, then she was. The same woman from Taverna! Taverna! Taverna! Beautiful. Sophisticated. Wrists dripping blood from a vicious pair of slashes.

She looked at me and spoke. "Run for your life. I had no choice but to stay and die. Run before he cuts you, too." Her voice crackled like a bad radio signal. Not the apparition's body though; that signal was clear. By kitchen light, she was straddling the border between transparent and opaque. Unusual. Even Dead Cat, a more solid ghost than most, was see-through.

Not all apparitions are ghosts.

Two mouths had delivered a similar message. One of them —Betty's—was even reliable.

If she wasn't a ghost, what was she? Eva Vasiliko had some kind of out-of-body experience while she was unconscious. *Kyrios Harry's sister* had looked like a ghost in every respect. I could see the wall through her. She'd had issues with furniture. This was different.

"What is it?" Leo said. He was staring at me. Worried.

The second woman appeared. No shimmer. Pantyhose looped around her neck. Pretty but purple from having the life squeezed out of her. Every bit as dense in texture as her friend. She opened her mouth to speak.

I held up my finger. "Don't say anything."

Leo sat back in his chair. "Okay ..."

He had misunderstood, of course.

I stomped into the living room, where the Marias were milling around the television, watching *Clueless*. *Kyrios* Harry was by the window, for a change.

"Kitchen. Now."

The Marias weren't happy about leaving the couch but they straggled into the kitchen behind *Kyrios* Harry.

"Who do you see in here?" I asked the dead people. Ghosts could see other ghosts, and these ghosts had been able to see Kyria Eva's apparition before she woke up. Could they see the matching pair of alleged murder victims?

Leo looked up. "You."

"Not you," I said. "I'm asking them."

His forehead crumpled up. He took another stab at the fries.

"I see sexy man," one of the Marias said, "and he is eating *tiganites*. I miss *tiganites*."

"You never ate *tiganites* when you were alive," another Maria told her.

I turned to *Kyrios* Harry.

He shrugged. "I see a man and you. Nobody else."

"Okay, you can go," I said.

Leo pushed away from the table. "If that's what you want."

My Virgin Mary ... "Again—not you."

He hovered between sitting and standing, clearly confused.

I turned to the two apparitions, who were casually dying all over again in my kitchen, and pointed my fork at them. "You two are not ghosts. What are you?"

They quit dying and took up giggling, clinging together against the kitchen wall. "Awww! It's less fun if he knows you can see us," they said in unison.

"Get out of my house." I jabbed my fork at them.

"But we like it here with him," the bleeder said. "He belongs to us."

There was a low growling from the other room. Something large and marmalade flew into the room and launched itself at the women in a clatter of claws and hissing. The apparition women shrieked. They fell backward, through the kitchen wall, and vanished. Dead Cat sat on the patch of floor they'd just vacated. Satisfied with his hunting skills, he lifted a back leg and began licking his balls.

A cold sweat drenched my skin. Shaking, I braced my hands against the tabletop. Sat.

"What just happened?"

"More crazy. I'm really tired of crazy. I need to vomit and sleep—in that order."

Leo inspected me across the table. His face was grave and concerned. "I'm taking you to the hospital."

"It's the food," I said. "Crusty Dimitri's is poison. I'll be fine. You can go."

"Are you talking to me this time?"

"Yes."

"I'm not going anywhere until I know you're okay."

He scooped me up like I was a feather, carried me to the bedroom, sat me on the edge of the bed and pulled my boots off as though I was a little kid. Then he swiveled me around and tucked me in.

"Is your couch comfortable?"

I thought about the Marias lined up across the cushions. He'd never know they were there.

"You don't have to stay."

"Yes," he said, "I do."

———

Leo was gone the next morning but he had left a note.

"It says he has gone to meet with the Thessaly Police," *Kyrios* Harry said.

"Don't read my mail."

"It is not mail, it is a note. An unfolded note, sitting on your desk, where anyone could read it."

"Ghosts," I muttered.

"We are dead. Our options are limited."

So Leo was meeting with the Thessaly Police. What would become of *Kyria* Eva? Would they treat her like a suspect or victim? I hoped they would have more luck than I did. As far as suspects went, I hadn't managed to rule out anyone definitively.

Penny Papadopoulo didn't strike me as a killer. She seemed satisfied that she had made Harry eat wood and sent him on his way.

Eating wood is a spanking. Sometimes it's a sex thing and sometimes it's not.

As for Angela, I believed her. Opening a supermarket on Merope, just so she could stock Royal Pain bread was the most Angela thing ever. So was her fretting that everyone on the island would hate her for it. The woman needed a therapist. What she had was a bunch of servants and me.

Johnny Margas was still a candidate. As *Kyrios* Harry's secret brother-in-law, he stood to benefit directly from Harry's death. His wife would inherit the Royal Pain business. If he had succeeded in snuffing her with that pillow, he would now be the sole heir of the Royal Pain company. He wouldn't need Wundebar Bread. Johnny Margas was about to become that child from the Bible, the one with two mothers, except instead of mothers he had two different police departments yanking on his arms.

I sat at my desk and opened my mail. The few jobs waiting were small but they all contributed to Finder Keepers' bottom line. I would never be rich but that was okay, especially now that I owned my own place. I found coveted trinkets, sorted out a family squabble by finding a solution the siblings couldn't see, and let a perennial client from the mainland know that her "missing" daughter was still alive and well and working hard under her alias.

Procrastinating?

Who, me?

Definitely me.

Those two spooks last night had freaked me out. They weren't ghosts, so what were they?

Betty Honeychurch was the closest thing I had to an encyclopedia of the paranormal and weird, but it was too early to take my questions to the Cake Emporium. Later, I would be on Betty's doorstep, questions in hand. But first, I wanted to talk to a long-dead woman about closure.

My phone rang.

"Sorry I had to leave," Leo said. "What are you doing?"

I told him I was on my way to Merope's Best for a steaming cup of punishment and regret.

He chuckled, then he turned serious. "We need to talk. Tonight. Dinner at my place. Any questions?"

"Are we having Crusty Dimitri's again?"

"This body is a deadly weapon," he said. "Do you think I would fuel it with Crusty Dimitri's food three times in one year?"

"Can we really call it food?"

He laughed but there was tension in his voice. "I will see you tonight."

I showered and threw on jeans, layering a black sweater over a long-sleeved shirt. One pair of boots, a belt, and a ponytail holder later I was ready for the short walk to Merope's Best. The scorched beans hunkered down on top of last's night's ouzo and Crusty Dimitri's mystery meat, threatening to give me a wicked case of heartburn. I silenced it with a *kourabietha*. Those Greek shortbreads smothered in powdered sugar will cure almost anything.

Time to burn off the sugar.

I grabbed my bicycle from the apartment building's foyer and peddled up to the cliff, where the long-dead Maria Petsini was contemplating the churning water below.

"You again," she said, then fell.

I sat cross-legged on the ground and waited for her to *poof!* back into position.

One ... two ... three ... "You're still here?"

"Maria Petsini?"

She blinked. "I know that name." Her forehead scrunched like cheap toilet paper. "I was that name, wasn't I?"

"You went missing twenty years ago."

"Missing ..." She touched her collarbone, lost in thought. "I left something behind. I know I did. What was it?"

"Your parents?"

"My parents ... are they still alive?"

"I think so. They offered a reward for information, but there wasn't any. If anyone knew what happened to you, they didn't speak up."

"I remember," she said. "I was working on a yacht."

"Doing what?"

"A stewardess. I did everything my employer demanded, and I did it without complaint. My family thought I was studying at the university."

"You didn't tell them you were a stewardess?"

"Maybe I did. I don't remember. Has it really been twenty—"

No finishing that sentence. She fell again. Seconds later, there was a shimmer, a *poof!*, and she was back. "I keep doing that," she said. "I never mean to but it happens."

A dark thought blossomed. That was it. She couldn't stop jumping because she had never jumped in the first place. Was Maria was pushed to her death twenty years ago?

"You didn't jump? Maria, were you pushed?"

"Why would I jump? I had everything to live for." The grooves on her forehead deepened. "There was an argument ... and then I was in the water."

"An argument? With who?"

"I don't remember, or maybe I never knew. Would you do something for me?"

"Yes."

Before she could tell me, she fell again. Then, four seconds later, she popped back, dry and unruffled.

"Tell my family where I died. You are the first person to speak my name in twenty years. Maybe they will give you the reward."

———

I had nothing solid to give Maria Petsini's family. Telling them a ghost story wasn't evidence, it was grounds for a restraining order.

Did that stop me? Not for a minute.

I hunted down the family's phone number and called them, cool wind whipping my cheeks. Overhead the sun was shrugging shoulders it didn't have, saying, "You want heat? It's hot and sunny in Australia right now."

The Petsinis' phone was answered with a heavy male sigh and a single word. "Come." Standard Greek phone greeting, minus the sigh. I identified myself and asked if I could speak to him about his daughter Maria.

There was a long silence.

"Kyrios Petsinis?"

"It is impossible right now, no matter how much we wish it."

"Please. It's important. Can I come and speak with you? Would that be easier?"

"No. I am sorry. There has been a death in the family and we are in mourning. After forty days, then you may come see us, but before that we cannot receive you."

Greek funeral protocols. Wear black; head to toe for women; armbands for men because Greece embraces its double standards and hugs them tight. No socializing for forty days. The funeral doesn't count as socializing. Neither does the wake.

"When the forty days is over, I'll call. How many days is that from today?"

He hung up without ceremony ... or words.

I glanced at my phone. The Cake Emporium would be flipping the sign in the door to Open any minute now. Betty would be there with cake and information.

And she was. The cake was midnight black, thick black-berry jam spread between the layers. It tasted like some long lost summer.

"It's Halloween," she told me. "I doubt we will have any children come by for sweets, but we're prepared all the same." Either side of the door sat two enormous glass pumpkins, overflowing with candy, each generous piece wrapped in orange or black. If any of Merope's children did Halloween, the Cake Emporium would become the haul of legend.

"We? You mean you and your brother?"

Jack Honeychurch was responsible for every confection in the store. So far, I had not met the elusive Jack, nor had I spotted him around the island. The Honeychurches didn't get out much. Merope in winter wasn't exactly a thriving metropolis. Most people only poked their noses outdoors to load up on groceries and firewood. Gossip came to them through the phone and some magical communication system. A hive mind.

"Jack isn't one for people. He's shy. Has been since we were knee-high. But I'll be here handing out sweets to anyone who wants them. He made the candy bars, but I get the fun part, don't you think?"

I missed Halloween and the candy that went with it. Traipsing from house to house in costumes made for early September, not the end of October. Inspecting the loot after ward with my friends, stuffing ourselves with sugar until our bodies levitated. Halloween wasn't something I'd done as an adult. Handing out candy to cute kids was one of those opportunities I'd lost when my folks got tired of my grandmother faking imminent death and moved back to Greece.

"You're welcome to hand out sweets with me," Betty said. She inspected my face. "No, you have other plans, and that's why you're here, aren't you?"

Yikes. I didn't want her to think I was using her. I wasn't. Betty was one of my favorite people. "I'm also come here for the company and the cake. I don't need cake today though, sorry. You loaded me up yesterday."

Her laugh was a bright tinkling sound, delicate yet it filled the air. Like Tinker Bell, if Tinker Bell hadn't been suffering from unrequited love.

She reached across the table, patted my hand.

"You would have to work hard to offend me, luv. You've got a good heart. Even the work you do is about helping other people."

"For money."

"People don't help other people, even if it's for money, unless they've got a smidgen of goodness in them. You've got more than a smidgen. Your center is gooey caramel." Elbows on the table. Chin in hands. Eyes on me. "Now, tell me what you saw."

I laid it out for her. The date. The dead women. My escape through Taverna! Taverna! Taverna!'s bathroom window. Their encore performance in my kitchen last night.

"It sounds to me like that policeman of yours has picked up a problem or two," she said when I was done.

"What are they? They're not ghosts."

"Definitely not ghosts, although they're pretending to be. Two women, putting on a show about how they were either murdered or offed themselves, trying to scare you off.

Showing up when you finally get some alone time with your policeman. I bet they soiled their knickers when they realized you could see them."

"Both times there was food involved. Although I'm not sure Crusty Dimitri's can be called food."

"Of course." Her bright eyes clouded over. Gravity grabbed the edges of her lips and gave them a good tug. "Succubi. I detest succubi. They're worse than a bedbug infestation, and they seem to have attached themselves to the detective."

The contents of my head were on the spin cycle. Ghosts were real—okay. Most paranormal creatures were based on a speck of truth—also okay. But now succubi were, too? Before I'd walked in here my mind was open. Now it was just full.

"Three questions." I set the fork down and ticked them off on my fingers. "Why? How? Is there an exterminator for this kind of thing?"

She got up for a moment. When she came back there was a cup of hot chocolate in each of her hands. Underneath each cup, a saucer. Atop each saucer, surrounding the cup, were three kinds of fudge. I breathed deep as she sat them down. At least one of the fudges was loaded with whiskey.

"Succubi don't attach themselves to just any man. They're drawn to attractive men, men who naturally draw the female eye. They're like crows that way. They like pretty, shiny things and collect them where they can. And they don't like competition."

"They see me as the competition."

She sipped her hot chocolate and smiled into the cup. "Perfect every time. Yes, I'm afraid they see you as the competition. You're not." She looked at my face which had broken out in a rash of disappointment, despite me trying to keep a neutral mask, and gave me a motherly smile. "There, there. Your police detective has a great deal of interest in you.

How can those succubi possibly *compete*? He doesn't even know they exist."

My mood lifted slightly. "What do they do?" I scrounged through my memory banks for mentions of succubi. *Bram Stoker's Dracula*. Gary Oldman sporting wicked hair buns. Keanu Reeves and his stilted British accent, writhing around with women in period costumes from no time period ever.

"They are avid collectors of men, mostly. To most demons, people are collectables, like those Smurf figurines from the 1980s, or Charles and Diana's wedding memorabilia."

"Most demons," I muttered. "How do I get rid of them?"

"The succubi? You don't. That's up to your policeman, I'm afraid. That's why banishing a succubus is so difficult and annoying: most men don't realize they're part of a collection." She tapped her chin thoughtfully. "Although I suppose since you can see them, you might try asking them to naff off politely."

Naff off? That had to be a British thing. "Politely?"

"Most demons respond well to good manners. They're not all monsters."

"And if they won't go?"

"Then you'll have to help the detective see the light."

Tough. Too tough. Leo didn't believe in woo-woo things. He'd told me so with his own mouth.

"Maybe not," Betty said, reading my mind. "But he believes in you."

———

I spent the afternoon in the weak sun, sipping good coffee and clearing a couple of small jobs off my list. The Thessaly Police hopped on their boat late afternoon and sailed off into the sunset. They'd spent the afternoon combing over the wreckage of the Royal Pain and they had left a couple of their forensics guys behind to pick over the bones. As they were pulling out of port, Leo texted. Johnny Margas went with them. Eva Vasiliko was being transferred this afternoon.

Two suspects gone. My case, such as it was, had ground to to a halt, along with Leo's.

Sam called. "That garbage you gave me was clean."

"It was the bread," I said.

"You didn't give me bread."

"I didn't have any to give you."

"Always logical. I like that about you." He blew me a kiss. "You want to come over for dinner and bring dinner with you?"

"Can't. Not tonight."

"Woman, you better be blowing me off for a hot date."

"You know," I said, "I think maybe I am."

———

A good dinner guest is one who shows up with things like dessert or wine. Or, in my case, dessert *and* wine. For the second time that day I stopped at the Cake Emporium. Betty steered me toward tiny cakes she knew Leo would love.

"He has a secret Merenda habit," she told me as she lowered several sugary acorns into the box. "These are filled with hazelnut and praline. Trust me, he'll love these."

Next I stopped at the More Super Market for wine and selected a bottle of Assyrtiko from Santorini and and bottle of Muscat of Samos.

This evening, the Triantafillou brothers were sitting behind the counter while Stephanie Dola filed her nails. If they were bothered by her violation of the health code, it didn't show.

"Aliki Callas," the brothers crowed. "*Kaloste!*"

I accepted their welcome and wished them a good evening. "*Kalispera*, *Kyrios* Yiorgos, *Kyrios* Dimitri, Stephanie." Stephanie reluctantly pocketed the nail file. She scanned the wine, placed the bottles in plastic bags. She was moving slower than usual. I wondered if she'd had a chance to approach the elderly brothers about violating labor laws.

"We have a new product. You want to try it?" she said.

New products rarely came to Merope, so this was a momentous occasion.

"What is it?"

"Bread," Yiorgos Triantafillos said. "Harry Vasilikos's death is a tragedy, yes, but his business lives on, and so must ours."

Sure enough, a pile of Royal Pain bread was stacked between the Merenda and the olive oil.

"You were going to accept *Kyrios* Vasilikos's offer?" I asked him.

He leaned forward, both hands on his walking stick. "Harry was an old friend. We owed him a favor."

"What about Merope's bakers?"

They shrugged in unison. "Business is business."

A greasy spider tiptoed up my spine.

"Where did you get the bread?"

"The Thessaly Police brought it from Harry's yacht," Kyrios Dimitri explained. "It was our bread. We already paid him for it."

"Have you sold any yet?"

They looked to Stephanie like she was the holy mount, not a high school dropout whom they refused to pay properly.

Stephanie said, "What was the question again?"

"The Royal Pain bread, have you sold any?"

"Maybe. I don't remember."

"Think hard," I said. "It's important."

"Why?"

"Because there's a good chance the bread was poisoned."

Color bled out of her face, leaving her with two red stripes along her cheeks. Stephanie had never heard of things like blending and contouring.

"Virgin Mary," she whispered, crossing herself frantically. "I sold one loaf."

"Just one? Who bought it?"

"*Kyrios* Grekos. He said he was buying it because his mother would have hated sliced, packaged bread from a mainlander's factory."

Panos Grekos, Merope's coroner. He had dead mama issues. "When?"

She made a face that said she ran on Greek time—and badly. "Earlier."

I reached for my phone and called Leo.

"Tell me you're not calling to cancel our date," he said, voice deep and smooth.

"Postponing." I told him why I was calling. He cursed the Virgin Mary, his great-grandmother, three goats, and a pumpkin. Apparently he wanted them to do something sexual, anatomically impossible, and illegal in several American states. Lucky for him, Europeans were more broadminded. From the way he ended the call midstream, I knew he was racing to his car.

I told Stephanie and the Triantafillos brothers not to sell any more of the bread, then I paid for my wine and rode towards home. The night was alive with sirens—police and ambulance. Leo had mustered the cavalry.

New plan.

Go home. Ignore the cakes in the box. Ignore the wine. Drink ouzo instead. Grapple with the whole succubi thing. Hope for something sappy on TV.

Could I convince Harry Vasilikos and the Marias to hide

in the closet for a few hours? That way I could pretend they didn't exist.

Kyrios Harry didn't know yet that I was ditching his case. With Johnny gone and the Thessaly Police transferring his sister, there was nothing for me to do. The other suspects were scattered across Greece. He wouldn't be happy and I wouldn't get information about Andreas. Closure would be out of my reach forever.

The question was, could I live with that?

I dismounted at the curb. *Kyrios* Yiannis was there with a Greek leaf blower, also known as a broom.

"Smile," he said.

"Do your job," I said. He grinned and kept sweeping. I continued through the courtyard, then stopped.

"If I wanted to get rid of you, how would I do it?"

"You want to get rid of me?"

"No. It's hypothetical."

"I don't know what that means."

The dead gardener came from a generation that eschewed education above the grade school level.

"It means it's pretend."

"Pretend, eh? Let me think." He rested his hands on the handle of the broom for a moment. "Find out what I hate and do that."

"What do you hate?"

"Turks."

Kyrios Yiannis was also from a generation that believed Turks were the devil. Forced occupation will do that to people.

"I don't think *Kyrios* Harry cares about Turks," I said.

"But he cares about something, I guarantee it."

With that in mind, I jogged upstairs with the wine and cakes, not even remotely relieved that I didn't have to get prettied up for my date with Leo. Succubi or not, now that I knew he wasn't a serial killer, certain body parts were hot for him again. Mostly the ones below my hair and above my soles.

Across the hall, all was quiet. No German pop. No *Kyria* Olga laughing about how she'd won Bingo again.

Grief welled up in me the way it always did these days. Maybe I should invite Lydia over for dinner. Dust off my cooking skills and conjure up something sturdier than a sandwich. We could share funny stories about *Kyria* Olga, or pretend she'd gone on a vacation to Mykonos, hunting for old men in Speedos. Whatever worked to quell the sadness. Not tonight, but soon.

I tried turning the key but my door was already unlocked. Strange.

Moving slowly, I nudged the door open with my toe until it was flat against the wall. My heart sped up. My mouth dried up. Different apartment, but the deja vu was blood curdling.

From the hall, everything appeared normal.

Almost everything. My living room was ghost-free. Maybe they were crowded around the bathroom mirror again. Vanity didn't die along with the human body.

"*Kyrios* Harry? Maria, Maria, Maria, Maria, and Maria?"

Footsteps on the stairs, then a voice. "Are you talking to yourself? You are, aren't you? Boy, you're *trela*, even for a giant."

Jimmy Kontos sat his child-sized *kolos* on the bottom step. He drew circles in the air beside his temples. The guy was a pain but his timing was convenient—convenient for me.

"Do me a favor," I said.

"Why should I?"

"Because if you don't, I'll steal your gold and your favorite axe."

He flipped me off. "You think you're funny, don't you?"

"I never joke about dwarves."

"What do you want?"

"Go into my apartment."

"Why? Is there a trap? Flour over the door? Water?"

"The door is open. Look: no flour."

He started up the stairs. "Forget it. I've got places to go and people to do."

"Thanks for nothing," I called out.

I peered into my apartment. Maybe the Harry and the Marias had moved on. Their remains were gone, bits of the yacht were currently on their way back to the mainland, and the only survivor was scheduled to be airlifted to a different hospital. It made sense that they had followed their bodies. Didn't it?

It was possible I'd forgotten to lock my door on the way out this morning. Wouldn't be the first time. Merope's underbelly was seedy and sinful, but robberies were not the island's crime of choice—not outside of tourist season anyway. The local criminal element considered it unGreek to steal from their neighbors, and on Merope we were all neighbors.

In I went, locking the front door behind me. The pepper spray I kept at the bottom of my bag came out.

"Harry? Marias? Anyone here?"

Silence. Not even a meow.

"Dead Cat?"

One room at a time. No ghosts in the living room. Or the kitchen.

I eased into the bedroom, pressing the door fully open with my shoulder, pepper spray in hand and ready to make an intruder cry and blow snot bubbles. And there they were, Harry Vasilikos, the Marias, and my cat, huddled together inside a ring of salt. The salt shaker was on the bedside table.

Someone had trapped them. I kind of wanted to know how because it could be useful.

"Who did this?"

Kyrios Harry's mouth moved. Words didn't come out. Dead Cat was spitting and hissing but I couldn't hear that either.

I moved closer, lifted my boot, intending to break the circle.

Kyrios Harry pointed. His mouth opened wide. My cat hurled himself against the spiritual forcefield.

I pivoted on one foot, just in time to see the crispy visage of Eva Vasiliko swing my laptop.

She didn't miss. Neither did I.

I collapsed in a pile of my own snot bubbles and tears.

CHAPTER TWELVE

SOMEONE WAS CARRYING ME. Somebody big, warm, and strong who didn't mind snot. I knew this because he wasn't staggering and complaining about how I needed to invest in antihistamines. I felt my body being lowered onto a soft surface. My couch. Then a male voice said, "Hold out your arm."

"What for?" My voice was thick, the words fluffy and squishy. I sounded like I'd been having a week-long affair with a barrel of ouzo and huffing capsaicin.

"I need to apply the leeches."

Leeches?

My eyelids sprang open. It was him, the gothic novel escapee. As always, he was in black. It suited him. No—it *was* him. A second skin.

"No leeches," I said.

He was smiling. The leeches were a joke—to one of us, anyway.

"What happened?"

"You were assaulted," he said.

Details came back. The salt prison. *Kyria* Eva. Pepper spray. My laptop.

My *laptop*. I groaned.

My entire life was on that machine. Backed up to a couple of clouds, sure, but it would take time to set everything up again. I wiped my eyes with the back of my hand. Flecks of my computer's case rained down like confetti. *Kyria* Eva was a twig but she swung like she was in the major leagues.

Questions jostled to be first in line.

Why had she knocked me out? Had she escaped from the hospital or slipped the police? How did she convince the ghosts to stand still while she built a salt cage around them? Could she see them? Where was she now?

"Why are you here?"

The man in black brushed his hand across my hair. More bits of plastic fell away. His hand was hot and gentle. I closed my burning eyes and reveled in the aroma of good vanilla and expensive whiskey.

My eyes popped open. "Are you a ghost?"

"No."

"Do you have a name?"

"Several."

"Could you give me one?"

"You should see a doctor."

Pain spidered out from my forehead as I winced. Now would be a good time to reconsider bangs. "I'll be fine."

His hand moved south to cover the burgeoning goose egg. Heat spread across my skin, through my bones.

"What are you doing?"

"Close your eyes."

Happy to.

A long moment later, he pulled his hand away. The pain was gone.

And so was he.

———

Leo didn't answer his phone, so I left a message. Next I called the police station and told them Eva Vasiliko was on the loose.

"We'll send someone over," Constable Pappas said. "And given that I'm the only one here, it will probably be me."

"Stay away from my underwear drawer."

He made a disappointed sound.

I walked softly through my apartment and carried a big stick. Well, a broom. No trace of *Kyria* Eva or her freakishly strong right arm. Hopefully someone would notice a burn victim streaking through the streets of Merope, wearing a hospital gown.

The ghosts were still surrounded by salt. Their faces ranged from grim to furious. I whisked through the ring with the broom. Dead Cat made like a cannonball and shot out. The others wobbled out more slowly.

"Your sister is a *skeela*," I told *Kyrios* Harry. A she-dog.

His expression said he had serious regrets when it came to penning his Last Will and Testament. "Eva is as strong as the shell of an egg and as cunning as a sloth. I guarantee this was not her idea."

"How did she get you into the circle?"

One of the Marias spoke up. "She made up a story about how none of us were really dead, and if we wanted to wake up, we had to stand still while she sprinkled the salt."

"And you believed her?"

"I didn't believe her," another Maria said.

I swept the rest of the salt into a pile. "I told you you were dead—all of you except *Kyria* Eva."

"We forgot," the first Maria said.

The other Maria rolled her eyes. "I didn't forget."

"You were in that circle, too," I pointed out. "You got in there somehow."

Those rolling eyeballs of hers found a place to land, on the floor. I looked down. Sometimes a floor is just a floor. This was one of those times.

"You were talking to her in the living room," one of the other Marias said to the eye-roller. The rest of the gaggle nodded.

"She said if I did not get in the circle, she would go to the hospital and kill us all."

The other Marias crossed themselves dramatically. Prayers were said.

Kyrios Harry snorted. Sentimentality wasn't his thing.

"Most people can't see ghosts," I said. "How was she talking to you if she couldn't see you?"

My phone rang. Betty Honeychurch was on the other end.

"You shot the question up into the sky, so I couldn't help seeing it. I hope you don't mind. Your *Kyria* Eva walked next to death and her soul traveled, appearing in your apartment, so it wouldn't be surprising if she could see the dead, even now that she's awake."

"I don't suppose you know where she is?"

"No, luv. Wherever she is, her head is as silent as the grave."

She blew me a kiss and hung up.

There was a knock on my door, followed by another. A rhythmic tapping. Some wiseass was trying to do a super-secret knock.

Constable Gus Pappas waved at me through the peephole. "I promise I won't look through your underwear this time."

I opened the door. At the same time, Lydia emerged from 201. She was dressed to kill and get off scot-free. Pappas puffed his chest out, tried to look cool. He touched his gun— the one on his hip. Another minute longer and he'd be hopping around like a Bird of Paradise in a David Attenborough documentary.

"Get in here," I said to him.

Lydia's glossy grin reached her eyes. "I see you have a thing for law enforcement."

"Break-in," I said.

Her grin fell away. "What are you doing?"

All these years on Merope and I still twitched when people used "What are you doing?" for "How are you?" I twitched when I did it, too.

"I'm okay—now."

"Let me know if you need anything," she said.

Off she went, hips swinging. Pappas watched her until there was nothing left of her but perfume.

"Wow," he said.

I held my finger to my lips. "Watch this," I whispered, pointing to the stairs. Sure enough, Jimmy Kontos came trotting down. The rotten little shrimp extended his middle finger and scratched his nose on the way past.

"Bring me back some candy from the Wonka factory when you're finished singing about naughty children for the day," I called out.

"Go choke on a beanstalk," he yelled back.

"You two are strange." Constable Pappas followed me inside. "Talk to me about that woman."

"She hit me over the head with my computer. When I woke up, she was gone."

"Not her," he said, picking up my few ornaments and setting them back down again. "We already know Eva Vasiliko escaped. I meant your neighbor."

I rolled my eyes. "Get in line."

"There's a line?"

An image of Jimmy Kontos popped into my head. He was hiding in the bushes. "A short one."

"Is she single?"

"Let's just say she's generous with her affection."

"I like generosity and I like affection." The constable grinned. "Could you tell her about me?"

"I could but I'm not going to unless you do your job."

He grimaced. "There is always a catch. Okay, show me where it happened."

Gus Pappas spent the next ten minutes wandering around my apartment, taking photos. He spent a lot of time in my bedroom. I went in to find him taking pictures of my underwear.

"Pappas!" I barked.

He leaped back.

I wagged my finger at him. "What did I say?"

"Something about not touching your underwear. But I'm not touching it. I'm just taking photos." He nodded to the corner of my bedroom, where I'd swept the salt in to a small hill. There hadn't been time to scoop it into the dustpan. "Cooking in the bedroom?"

"Ever read the Bible?"

"Not today."

"That's the last man I caught taking pictures of my underwear."

"You look in a woman's underwear drawer one time—"

"Twice."

"Okay, okay. Twice. Are you going to tell Detective Samaras?"

"Are you going to shut the drawer and delete those photos?"

He quickly changed the subject. "How did Eva Vasiliko get in? And why do you think she came here?"

I didn't have answers to either question and I told him so. He took pictures of the door and windows, then he left, casting longing glances at apartment 201 on the way out.

Alone again.

I went to the kitchen for a medicinal shot of ouzo. As I was pouring, my eye caught something. Or rather, nothing.

Kyria Eva had stolen my wine, two boxes of cakes, and all my sandwich fixings.

———

Merope isn't a big island. There are a limited number of hiding places, including several sea caves that are impossible to get to without a boat, a low tide, and prayer. Every other summer, a tourist goes exploring and discovers one of more of the caves, despite abundant warnings that our caves are bad tempered and homicidal. Most of the time they make it back. Sometimes they don't, and a rescue team has to wait for the tide to ebb before they can haul the body or bodies back to dry land.

There was no way *Kyria* Eva could be in the caves. The tide was high and the island's rental boats were moored for the winter. Plus the police were on the lookout and the rental places would have been their first target. Wherever Kyria Eva was hiding, it was somewhere dry and sheltered.

I saddled up and went in search of my missing booze, food, and cakes. You don't just steal a woman's wine and cake and expect to get away with it. Plus she'd destroyed my laptop.

Crispy or not, Kyria Eva was going down, and I was going to be the one to do it.

It was personal.

For the next two hours, I took a tour of the island, one we keep secret from tourists. Abandoned houses. The shell of *Ayia* Paraskevi—Saint Friday—cracked by one of the region's myriad earthquakes. Old factories and warehouses, crumbling and stinking of rotted olives. The fruit was long gone but the stench was part of the concrete and wood.

I talked to people, ghosts, myself.

No sign of Eva Vasiliko.

Merope's main road was mostly empty. The few people out and about were bustling home or rushing to dinner at one taverna or another. When Greeks eat dinner in summer, it's a late meal that can stretch for several hours, long past midnight. But Merope in winter was a more conservative creature. Dinners happened early by Greek standards so everyone could take to their living rooms, where the wood burning ovens heated their homes via the long ventilation pipes that ran across the ceiling and out the exterior wall.

Old Vasilis Moustakas was standing the middle of the road, eyes fixed on the road. They lit up as I approached and stopped.

"What are you doing?" I asked him.

"You want to hear a joke?"

"Is it your *poutsa* again?"

He put on his best offended face. "No!"

"Is it sex with my *yiayia?*"

Cackle. "There was nothing funny about sex with your *yiayia.*"

I shrugged. "Okay, tell me. I like jokes."

"Why did the chickens cross the road?"

"To get to the other side?"

He laughed. "I don't know."

"*Kyrios* Moustakas?"

"What?"

"Your joke wasn't funny or a joke."

"But they are funny. Look, here they come again."

What do you know, the chickens really were crossing the road. At least a thousand of them rushing past, feathers ruffled, red combs flopping around, polluting the quiet night with their clucking. One at a time, they vanished as they reached the other side.

"That is a lot of dead chickens," *Kyrios* Moustakas said.

He was right. "Have you seen them before?"

"Only tonight. Hey, Aliki Callas, you want to see something?"

I rolled my eyes and got back on my bicycle. Roaming packs of ghost chickens weren't normal, for Merope or for me. Most of the time, dead animals stayed dead. Something was bugging me about these particular chickens. There weren't many chicken farms on the island, and only one was a thousand chickens strong. The Hondrou family's farm.

Virgin Mary help me, I did not want to encounter *Kyria* Hondrou's monobrow in the dark. I don't spook easily but that thing was the stuff of nightmares. Still, it couldn't hurt to swing by the farm and see if they were missing some chickens —or all of them.

At the Hondrou farm, the lights were on and Constable Pappas was parked out front. He was sitting behind the wheel of his police car, hands braced against the steering wheel, muttering to himself.

I tapped on the window. "Pappas?"

He rolled the window down. "Don't make me go in there. Please. Don't make me go in there."

"Is it the eyebrow?"

He shuddered. "I have nightmares about that thing. When I was a boy, my parents used to tell me if I played with my *poutsa* too much I would grow one just like it."

"You know you're a policeman with a big gun, yes?"

"A gun would not work against that eyebrow. Only fire." He looked up at me. "Why are you here?"

"I was just riding past," I lied. "Why are you here?"

"More than a thousand dead chickens."

So the dead chickens did originate at the Hondrou farm. "What happened?"

"Eleni Hondrou called half an hour ago to tell me the chickens were all dead. I heard the eyebrow screaming in the background." His expression was imploring and pitiful. "Come with me?"

"Forget it. I'm not going anywhere near that eyebrow."

The night shattered with one word: "YOU!"

Gus Pappas slid down in his seat. He crossed himself repeatedly. "My God, she found me."

Kyria Hondrou was hobbling across the yard, arm outstretched, finger pointy and accusatory. And the person it was pointy and accusatory at was me.

"YOU!"

I pointed to my own chest. "Me? What did I do?"

"Uh-oh," Constable Pappas said, "now you're done for. The eyebrow is going to get you."

Kyria Hondrou whacked the police car's hood with her cane. "You killed my chickens!"

Huh? "I didn't touch your chickens!"

She touched a claw to her eye. "You put the evil eye on them, you cursed them, and now they are all dead. I demand compensation. Where is that policeman?" She whacked the hood again. "I can see you hiding in there. Get out. Arrest her if she will not pay!"

Constable Pappas angled out of his seat. He was quaking in his black uniform. "I can't arrest her without evidence."

"What evidence do you need? My chickens are dead and just yesterday she was here."

"Do you have a murder weapon, *Kyria* Eyebrow? I mean Kyria Hondrou."

I gawked at him. *Kyria* Hondrou sucked her breath in—hard. Her black eyes gleamed in their potholes. The monobrow formed a dip, right in the center above her sharp nose.

The constable was pale. I understood; that eyebrow gave me the willies, too.

"What weapon? It was a curse, I told you."

Pappas cut his gaze to me. "Come with me."

"Where are you taking her? To jail?" Kyria Hondrou asked with unbridled glee.

"I need to see these chickens," he said.

"For what? I already told you they are dead."

He ignored her, tilted his head at me. I followed Pappas to the chicken yard, where easily a thousand chickens had met their maker, scattered and in clumps. They had died before roosting time.

"What do you do with these chickens?" Pappas threw the question over his shoulder to *Kyria* Hondrou, who was stumping along behind us. There was no sign of Eleni, her husband, or any of the Hondrou grandchildren. Probably they were hiding from the family matriarch's wrath.

"Who is this *vlakas*?" she asked no one in particular. "Who is your family? Do I know them? Are they good people? Do they know you are a *vlakas*?"

"They know," Constable Pappas said cheerfully. "Now can you answer the question please?"

"What does anyone do with chickens? We cut off their heads and people buy them to eat."

Hands on hips, Pappas surveyed the chickens. "So whoever killed them was doing you a favor, yes?"

Those black beads in her matching face-holes glittered dangerously. "No. No favor. I like to kill them myself."

Yikes! I started backing up, hoping to make a quick getaway. Her cane jumped out and snapped me behind the knees. "Where are you going? You killed my chickens."

"Why would I kill your chickens?"

"Jealously. Spite. What else could kill them this way except a curse?"

Pappas and I looked at the chickens. Dead chickens, with no visible signs of death except death. "What killed them?" he asked me.

"You're asking me? I don't know anything chicken physiology."

"It was a curse," *Kyria* Hondrou said, pounding her cane on the ground. "And it was her."

I turned to Pappas. "It wasn't me. You were at my place earlier, you know I was home and not out killing chickens."

Kyria Hondrou fixed her monobrow on me. "You. First you try to steal from me, then you curse my chickens. Now you are also a *putana*, entertaining this one in your bedroom?" She spat on the ground. "*Skoupidia*." Garbage.

"I don't think she likes you," Constable Pappas said.

Garbage, my kolos. Okay, Yiayia was free and easy with her affections, but my family wasn't garbage. And at least we didn't have that facial hair problem swimming in our gene pool, like some kind of hideous eel.

"You know what?" I said.

The old woman grinned. "Why you do not tell us, Garbage Girl?"

Okay, I'd had enough. More than enough.

"I'm thirty-one—"

"Old. A spinster And who would marry you anyway, Garbage Girl?"

My eye twitched. "I have my own business, my own apartment, and ..." I looked around "... and this bicycle. I don't have to stand here and listen while you fling lies about me and accuse me of chicken murder!"

I got on my bicycle.

"Where you think you are going, eh?" *Kyria* Hondrou shoved her cane between my rear tire's spokes. Nowhere. Apparently I was going nowhere.

"Do not leave me," Pappas pleaded.

This was ridiculous. I reached into my bag for my phone. My intention was to call Leo. This situation called for a policeman who was more police-y than Constable Pappas. Someone who wasn't afraid of Kyria Hondrou and her monobrow of horror.

Kyria Hondrou zeroed in on my hand. "What are you doing? You going to pull some kind of gun on me? Get off that bicycle and give me that bag." She snatched it off my shoulder, stuck her hand inside and began rifling around.

I heard her fingernails clank against something metal, then she grinned. "I will show you what happens to chicken killers. Give me a moment. What is this?" She had found my pepper spray. "Why you carry hairspray? You wear your hair like a hippie. Boring. No wonder you have no husband."

"Duck," I told Pappas.

"Why duck?" the old woman said, twisting the pepper spray in her hand. "What does this do?"

I heard the canister hiss, and then *Kyria* Hondrou emitted a blood-curdling shriek. Her howls dragged her family out of the house. Constable Pappas fell to his knees.

"Make it stop," he cried.

The neighborhood was typical for this part of Merope. Narrow streets. Dirt roads. White houses butted up to white houses, the exception being a few larger pieces of property, like the Hondrou farm. The neighbors couldn't resist the siren call; someone was in pain and they wanted to know every little detail. What they didn't learn they would make up, changing the story slightly with every retelling. They came fast—mostly because they'd been perched behind their shutters since Constable Pappas pulled up in his police car, waiting for the perfect moment to strike.

"What happened?" Eleni asked me.

"Pepper spray," I said.

Her lips quirked. "Awful." Her face said no, not awful at all. "You should go before she stops howling."

"I didn't kill the chickens."

"I know."

My adrenal gland told me to run, so that's what I did. I scooped up my bag, kicked *Kyria* Hondrou's cane out of my spokes and peddled until I couldn't hear her screams anymore.

Back at my apartment, I showered to get the stink of chickens out of my hair. Being in close vicinity to the birds, dead or not, had revived yesterday's stench. I swapped clothes for flannel pajamas and went to the kitchen, where I realized my cupboards and refrigerator were still bare. I had two choices: starvation or Crusty Dimitri's.

Only one of those two things could kill me.

Starvation was the safer choice.

———

It was after midnight when Leo called.

"Gus didn't eat the bread," he said. "And we confiscated every loaf from the More Super Market and the Super Super Market. The Triantafillos brothers were not happy. They asked to be compensated."

"That sounds like them. What did you say?"

"That if they didn't quit complaining, I would tell every baker in the village that they colluded with Harry Vasilikos to put them out of business."

I winced. Leo had thumped them in the wallet.

"I'm sorry about our date," he said. "And I'm even more sorry about Eva Vasiliko. How are you?"

"My laptop is dead. Apparently bone beats electronics. Now I need a new computer."

"We haven't found her yet, but we will. When we do, I'll make sure she replaces it for you, one way or another."

I told him about the missing groceries. "She's probably hiding somewhere, eating cake and drinking wine. How did she escape?"

"Ceiling, just before the Thessaly Police transferred her. Those squares are light and flimsy."

"So I suppose she's the main suspect?"

"It looks that way. As the beneficiary of her brother's business, she stands to gain the most from his death, along with Margas."

Conversation trailed off for a moment. Sleep tapped my shoulder, and I yawned.

"Have you eaten?" Leo asked me.

"No."

"What are you doing right now?" His voice was low, serious, and kind of sexy.

"*Kyria* Eva emptied my cupboards, so I'm dying of starvation."

He laughed. The warmth of that sound stirred my estrogen. "As a policeman it's my duty to not let you die. Come upstairs. I'll make you glad you're losing sleep."

"I'm in my pajamas."

"So take them off."

Yowza.

————

I swapped my pajamas for yoga pants and a sweater (both black) that grabbed my breasts and said, "Look at us!" And Leo did look when he opened the door. Hard and for a long time.

"Jimmy isn't home," he said, after a minute of appreciation.

"He's busy stalking Lydia."

Leo laughed. "Jimmy? Chase a woman?"

My own personal code of business conduct prevented me from telling him about Jimmy and the roses. "Why—is that weird?"

"Jimmy gets more women than—"

My eyebrows jumped into the judgmental position. "You?"

He grinned. "Than anyone."

I snorted in disbelief. "Jimmy? Jimmy Kontos. This high." I held my hand out. "Hairier than all of 80s porn combined? That Jimmy?"

"In some circles, he's a legend."

"Are these circles small?"

Leo laughed and pulled me into his apartment. This was my first time inside 302. Last time I'd stood in the doorway and accused Leo of having a revolving bedroom door. That's when I discovered he worked out at home. Tonight, his gym equipment was neatly stacked against the wall. His place was cozy, considering two men lived here. Plush rug under the couch and coffee table. Big, comfortable furniture. Bookcase overflowing. Someone had a serious reading habit. That same someone owned a television almost as big as the wall.

"Where does Jimmy sleep? In a drawer?"

"Couch."

I eyed the couch. It was more like a love seat. Too small for Leo to stretch out, but big enough to fit two Jimmys.

Leo saw when my mind was going. "It folds out into a bed. Still hungry?"

My stomach growled audibly. Yikes. If I didn't feed it soon there would be a revolt.

"What's for dinner?"

He opened the oven to show me a round pan of *spanako-pita*—spinach and feta pie. "Sit," he told me. "Be comfortable."

"I had wine," I said wistfully. "Nice wine. And I had cakes. Little hazelnut filled cakes."

"I have wine."

"Too late. Give me wine now and I'll fall asleep."

Leo dished up generous wedges of spanakopita, chunks of bread, pork souvlaki on long steel skewers. Everything went on to the table with small dishes of *tzatziki* for slopping all over the meat.

He joined me at the table. That's when they showed up again—succubi. Stupid succubi, bleeding and suffocating all over a perfectly good meal. Stupid, gorgeous, painfully beautiful succubi. It wasn't fair. Nobody should look that good without photo-manipulation.

I sighed.

Leo looked up from his plate. "You're not a vegan, are you?"

"Omnivore." I eyed the succubi, the self-satisfied succubi. They were enjoying the part where I squirmed. I was over this. Too many people had their fingers in the pie that was my life. It was time to crack some knuckles. "I need to tell you something."

The bleeder looked at the choker. "Uh—oh. She is going to tell him about us."

Her friend patted her on the shoulder. "He will not believe her. They never do."

Bleeder didn't look sure. "Sometimes they do. Remember Cleopatra and Antony?"

They both winced.

I tore a piece of bread in two. "I know what you are and of course I'm going to tell him. But first I'm going to ask you politely to leave. So, please leave."

Leo frowned. "Allie?"

I waved my bread at him. "Wait."

The succubi put their pretty heads together for a

moment, whispering. I chewed on the bread while I waited. Leo watched me with a crumpled forehead.

"I'm not crazy," I promised him. He looked nothing like convinced. That's okay, I knew they were there and I wasn't crazy, thanks to Betty Honeychurch.

Bleeder delivered the verdict. "Let us think about it ... No. We like this one. He belongs to us."

"He is so pretty," her friend purred.

Why couldn't this be easy? "I asked nicely."

"Still no."

Fine. They wanted to play hardball. My attention swung back to Leo. I swallowed the bread and took a good slug of water to wash it down. Then I told him everything: about the succubi and how to banish them back to whatever hell they had sprung from. Most likely the actual Hell. Just because the Greek Orthodox Church didn't believe in a fire and brimstone hell, didn't mean it wasn't real.

He laughed.

And laughed.

And laughed some more.

I calmly munched bread and drank water and waited for him to take a breath. The succubi filed their nails.

"True story," I said when he stopped.

"Succubi?"

"Two of them."

"Don't they drink blood?"

"That's vampires."

"That is vampires," Bleeder confirmed. "Blood is gross."

Leo couldn't hear her, of course. "What do they want?"

"They collect men. You're basically part of a collection, like a stamp or a rock."

He made a face. Being compared to a collectible was obviously new to him. "What do these succubi look like?" No doubt he was thinking about that same Gary Oldman movie.

"Like they get paid by the hour."

Choker clutched her chest. "I think the human woman just called us *putanas*."

The other one looked less offended. "An expensive *putana* or a cheap one? Because there is a difference."

"Whichever one won't leave when it's over," I said.

"Ooooh, she's jealous," Choker said.

"I'm not jealous," I snapped. "I'd just like to have one date without an audience."

Choker gave her demonic friend a knowing look. "She is jealous."

Enough was enough. These two were cutting into my food and sleep time.

"My Virgin Mary, just ask them to go," I told Leo.

The succubi tittered. "Oooooh, she will not help you, that one," Choker said. "Terrible hearing and a big ego."

Leo raised his eyebrows. "Ask them? Don't I need a priest or a bucket of holy water?"

The succubi hissed. For a split second they lost their candy coatings, revealing a glimpse of their icky centers. Underneath, they resembled raw veal schnitzel after a good pounding and a week under the July sun. The bile in my stomach made vague threats about how it would like to come out and spray them. I crammed another bite of bread into my mouth and triple-dog-dared it to try.

"How about we start with good manners and work our way up to exorcist," I said once the nausea had abated.

Leo glanced around. "Where are they?"

"Standing beside us. One of them is bleeding on the souvlaki."

The succubus looked at her wrists. "Sorry. I forgot to stop bleeding." The wounds vanished. "This is the first time in a thousand years anyone has seen us. We are not used to props."

Choker blinked and her pantyhose noose vanished. "They were fun though."

So help me, Virgin Mary, it was almost impossible not to roll my eyes at them. On the outside they were women, but on the inside they were teenage girls ... and also hideous monsters.

"Just do it so we can eat," I told the cop.

Leo shrugged and turned in his seat. It was clear he was humoring me, but I appreciated the effort. Later, I knew, there would be a discussion about my sanity. When that happened I would take him to meet Betty. "Can you leave, please? Dinner is getting cold again," he said.

The succubi huddled together again. "He did say please," Choker said.

Bleeder wasn't convinced. "But how do we know he really wants us to go? He is following her orders. Perhaps she has him in some kind of thrall. The human obviously has some kind of powers if she can see us."

For crying out loud, were these two clowns or demons?

Trick question; clowns are demons dunked in greasy makeup.

"Nobody wants a pair of demons following them around, watching them sleep and shower and eat," I told them, because they seemed to be struggling with the decision-making process.

Leo's eyebrows took a hike. "They watch me sleep?"

"We watch him do everything," Choker said.

Bleeder nodded. "Everything."

"Don't you have other men to stalk?" I asked.

"Of course. But we are demons, and we can be in a million places at once."

Interesting. One of my few remaining shreds of skepticism took a backseat. "How?"

"We exist in a pocket dimension."

I had questions—so many questions—but I also had dinner. I wanted food more than I wanted answers. Also, the sandman was creeping around, flicking sand in my face. It was already tomorrow and I was out of fuel and patience.

"He asked nicely," I said, "so go back to your cozy little pocket dimension and leave him alone. Find someone else to collect. There are lots of nice men out there. The world is filled with them."

"We have not decided yet," the succubi said in one voice.

They sat on Leo's small sofa and watched me watching them. Later I'd be hoofing it back to the Cake Emporium, shopping for more cakes and a way to banish these succubi—one without good manners, if that's what it took. Hopefully Betty would know a way.

I sighed and cut the spanakopita on my plate with the edge of my fork.

Across the table, Leo was watching me, fork and bread poised. "Did they leave?"

"They're on the sofa, watching us eat."

He ate in silence for a moment. He spent the time formulating a question. "Does this happen a lot?"

"I didn't know succubi existed until yesterday."

"And ghosts?"

"Ever since I can remember."

"How's the food?"

"Perfect."

"You want to go into my bedroom and make out?"

"Yes, please."

He grinned, slow and sexy. "Crazy or not, I want you."

Crazy. The word poured ice cold water over my libido, leaving it soggy and shivering.

"I'm not crazy."

"That's not—"

Leo's phone butted into the conversation. He got up to

answer, his words low and urgent. When he came back, his physique and face had shifted back into cop mode.

Our date was over. It was written all over him. Big letters. Practically graffiti.

"What is it?"

"They've found Eva Vasiliko."

"Great," I said. "I'm billing her for my laptop. She gets a pass on the groceries because probably she was hungry after being in a coma."

"You can't." Leo paused. His face was grim. "Eva Vasiliko is dead."

CHAPTER THIRTEEN

I NAPPED for five delicious minutes in Leo's car. He tried to leaving me behind, making all kinds of excuses about how civilians couldn't show up to a crime scene; but in the end I reminded him that he thought I was crazy, and crazy people are capable of anything. When I woke up, it was in a blaze of flashing lights. The island's emergency vehicles were huddled around the dock. We were near the top of the island, down a short distance from Maria Petsini's falling point but high enough for the drop to be deadly.

Leo's face was a smooth cop mask. "Stay here."

"Okay."

I didn't stay there. As soon as he got out, I followed. The paramedics were loading a bodybag into the ambulance.

"What happened?" Leo asked Constable Pappas.

"She jumped."

The rocks below were jagged teeth. Real man-eaters.

"Witnesses?"

"None. But she left a note and a check."

I tapped Pappas on the shoulder. "Who is the check for?"

Leo swung around. "I thought I told you to stay in the car."

"You did, but I'm not good at taking orders I don't want to take."

"For you." Pappas went to hand me the check.

Leo snatched it out of his hand. "Evidence. Where's the note?"

Pappas passed it over. Leo shone his flashlight over the paper. I craned my neck to peek at *Kyria* Eva's last words. They were succinct and penned in a pretty hand. She didn't poison the bread. She knew who did, but they were already dead, so what was the point of giving up that person's name? She had jumped because her fact was burnt off, her husband was cheating, and she couldn't enjoy food. She was sorry about my laptop but had the wine and cakes were delicious, especially the pralines. It had been years since she had last eaten carbs and she had wanted to stuff herself before her big finale. She could work magic with a bobby pin, so breaking in was a snap. The salt circle was to shut the ghosts up while she robbed me of my food. Included, she wrote, was a check to replace everything.

Kyria Eva had jumped. Suicide not homicide. I knew this because she hadn't bounced back, begging me to solve her murder.

And with her note, she'd told me everything I needed to know to crack this case.

All along I'd assumed the killer left the boat. What if they'd gone down with the ship?

———

Greek time moved at any old speed. It didn't care about things like punctuality or promises or employment. Me, I ran on American time. That meant I did what needed doing, when it needed to be done.

Sleep could wait. Puffing clouds of steam through my nose and mouth, I jogged to the top of the island, where Maria Petsini was reenacting her murder. She fell and then popped back into position.

"Maria?"

She turned around. "You're back again. Did you contact my family?"

"You said you had everything to live for. Did that include children?"

Her features softened. "My baby."

"You had a daughter, yes?"

"Maria."

Maria was her mother's name and it was hers. And it was a third Maria's, too. It was right there in front of me when I'd dug up information on the missing woman, but I'd failed to make the connection. Maria's father even told me there had been a recent death in the family. Another failed connection on my part.

I couldn't do it, couldn't tell Maria that her daughter was dead and that there was a possibility she murdered Harry Vasilikos and the other Marias. Not unless I had proof. Why shatter a broken heart?

I left the ghost to her reenactment, my brain huffing and puffing, processing data.

The Marias. They had the collective brightness of a broken light bulb. On the outside anyway. But what if I had misjudged one of them? And why, if one of the Marias was a murderer, did she do it? Nobody does murder and mayhem for funsies; there is always a reason.

Back home, my door was locked. Everything in its place. Nobody lurking behind a door to whack me over the head. The

Marias were in front of the television, swooning over an old
Alain Delon movie with subtitles. Just for a change, Harry Vasilikos was at the window, watching the night and all its stars.

"Your sister is dead," I said. "I'm sorry."

He didn't turn around. "Don't be. I will see her
again soon."

"I have good news, too. I think."

"What is it?"

Ignoring the Marias' protests, I turned off the television,
sat on my coffee table, and faced them.

"One of you killed the rest of you."

Now *Kyrios* Harry was interested. "What? Impossible."

"And yet, you're all dead," I told him.

"I don't believe it," he said.

"Believe it."

"No. These women would not do that."

Oh boy. "Then get out of the living room because you're
annoying and in my way. Also, I would rather talk to the
Marias alone anyway."

"This involves my murder," *Kyrios* Harry said, all puffed up
and pompous.

"It leaves the living room or else it gets the salt again,"
I said.

He pointed a transparent finger at me. "I will leave, but
only because it might help you solve this case more quickly."

"Bedroom. Now," I barked.

He stormed into the bedroom, huffing and complaining. I
closed the door behind him, then went back to the Marias.

"One of you has a mother named Maria. Raise your hand
if you are her daughter."

They looked at each other, then they all raised their
hands.

"Not helpful," I muttered. "Which one of you poisoned
the bread? I know one of you did."

They lowered their hands.

Great. This was going nowhere fast. I was tired, I was hungry, I was sick of ghosts infesting my home.

"I don't know why or who, but I'm going to figure it out, and when I do there will be consequences."

"Is it that time of the month?" one of the Marias said.

"If you mean the ghost-busting time of the month, then yes." I stomped into the kitchen and invaded the spice rack. "Who is ready for some salt? I have three kinds, including one with garlic."

The Marias scattered. Curse words sprayed the room. They tried throwing things—my things—but they hadn't learned any tricks or taken their basic afterlife orientation class yet.

I left them to it. Even scattered they moved in a pack. There was no way for me to break bits off the herd for questioning.

There was another way to sort the Marias.

Sam was awake. Insomnia. He always said he didn't mind because he didn't want to waste a minute of Greece. Tonight he didn't grumble too hard when I asked him to run a search on the Petsini family—more specifically Maria Petsini the younger. There were limits to my search skills, especially now that I was missing a laptop. Moments later, I was staring at my phone, shaking my head.

"I thought you were magic."

"There's a limit to this awesomeness," Sam said. "I don't like it any more than you do. You know how many women in Greece are named Maria Petsini? A lot. You know when Greeks have to sign up for an ID card?"

"When they're twelve-years-old."

"Exactly. You know how long they're good for?"

"Fifteen years."

"You got it. So you've got me looking at pictures of kids

who all share the same name. You want more, it's gonna take time and cake."

"Cake I can do. I'm not sure about time."

"One out of two ain't bad."

———

I needed a who. I needed a why. There was only one avenue left to getting both.

Were the Thessaly Police coming to the same conclusions? Probably not. From the sounds of things they had shifted their investigation away from Merope to the Sporades. To them, Merope was a destination not an origin. And they had Johnny Margas, suspect Numero Uno. Maybe we would cross paths at some point; in the meantime, I was headed to the mainland for, I hoped, answers.

Black slacks. Black boots. Black sweater and coat. Mourning the dead was easier in winter when the black didn't transform the human body into a sweat machine.

At this time of year a ferry left for the mainland via Skiathos every morning. I had twenty minutes to spare, so I grabbed my bag and bolted.

Aboard the ferry, I stood on the upper deck and watched Merope vanish, frigid sea air swirling around me. I wasn't alone. A handful of ghosts spent their bottomless well of time taking the voyage between islands. They were quiet and so was I. Okay, not the former ferry captain with verbal diarrhea —him I ignored; too much ranting about Poseidon's penis— but the others were definitely quiet.

Once Merope was gone, I went inside and shivered for the next few hours, while I tried to figure out exactly what I hoped to get out of this trip.

Maria Petsini from the cliff had a mother named Maria Petsini and a daughter, also named Maria Petsini. Why was

Maria Petsini the younger on that boat, and why did she murder the Royal Pain's passengers, including herself? Which of the five Marias was she?

The eldest Maria Petsini and her husband were the only ones who could help.

Leo called. "Where are you?"

"On the ferry."

His frown traveled through the phone. "Why?"

"Work."

"Doily or missing person?"

"Missing doily."

"How about dinner when you get back?"

"No ..."

"Okay." He didn't sound okay with it.

"... at least not until I find out how to get rid of your other two dinner guests."

"The succubi."

I heard feminine giggling in the background, then, "Oooh, they're talking about us." My teeth gritted. Betty Honeychurch would be my first stop on the way home. Those succubi had to go.

"We'll talk when I get back," I said.

At Skiathos I switched ferries and continued on to Volos. From there it was a short bus ride to the village of Agria. Directions to the Petsinis' house came from the sour-lipped mouth of a living rock, who worked in a *peripetero*—a boxy news stand, conventionally manned by veterans.

"Are you here for the funeral?" he asked me.

"Yes."

He nodded. "Very sad, that accident. Maria was a good girl. She never made fun of my arm."

"Your arm?"

He raised a stump. "My invisible arm. It matches my invisible leg."

"What happened?"

"I fell out of a tree and onto a Turkish soldier holding a chainsaw."

Yikes. Who knew war involved tree pruning? "I'm sorry."

"Why? You did not push me out that tree. Do you want to see my *poutsa*?"

"No!"

"Good. I do not have one to show you. The chainsaw took that, too."

I bought a small block of ION chocolate, thanked him for his help, and set off for the Yiorgos and Maria Petsini's house.

The Petsinis family lived in a three-layered house with a flat, unfinished roof. It was surrounded by other houses with unfinished roofs, all of them clinging to a steep hill. Rebar sprang from their tops. Washing lines were strung between poles. Television antennae watched the sky for signals. Like the gardens on Merope, these gardens were largely potted. Yards were concrete. Greeks didn't have the luxury of grass lawns. The street was capillary thin, the concrete cracked like an ancient sharp of pottery. Not a road for the claustrophobic; the houses felt like they were looming over me, judgmental and moments away from nagging me about how I didn't have a husband and five children.

I stood at the gate and called out to *Kyrios* and *Kyria* Petsinis.

Before long, a woman shuffled out in black slippers and a black housecoat, deep grooves in her face, worn down by rivers of grief. White hair floated around her head. There was a comb stuck it in but she didn't seem to know or care.

"What do you want? Money? Go away."

"*Kyria* Petsini?"

"How do you know my name?"

I introduced myself, offered her my condolences, wished her a long life.

"I want to die," she said. She pulled a potato peeler out of her pocket. "Kill me. My husband won't do it."

"Because I want to die, too."

Kyrios Petsinis joined us at the gate, a long stick of wire of a man, bent at the back. His hair was black. His mustache was epic in size and scope.

"I'm not here to kill either of you," I said.

"Too bad," *Kyria* Petsini said. "Go away."

"Go away," her husband said. They shuffled back to the house, broken.

"We spoke the other day," I called out. "I came here from Merope."

They stopped. Turned around.

Kyrios Petsinis made a face. "The one who asked about our daughter Maria, yes?"

"Yes."

"I hung up on you."

"It's important."

Kyrios Petsinis spend several long, silent moments weighing the situation. "Do you know our daughter Maria? Have you seen her? Do you know where she is? Or are you just here for the money? Most of the time they come for the money."

If I told them I could see the dead, they'd mistake me for a liar or worse.

(What's worse than a liar? Fake mediums and okra, alone or in the same dish.)

"I'm a private investigator, of sorts. I'd like to talk to you about the other Maria, too. Your granddaughter."

Kyrios Petsinis eyed me. "The other day you mentioned our daughter. You said nothing about our granddaughter. Which one is it?"

"Both. I believe your daughter died on Merope, and I

don't think it's a coincidence that your granddaughter also ended up there."

The grieving grandmother shot me a dirty look, speckled with hatred. Who could blame her? She had already lost so much. "The police said Maria was killed before the yacht crashed. We have already told them everything we know. What can a private investigator do for us? Nothing. And you are wrong about our daughter Maria. She is still alive." She pressed a fist to her chest. "I feel it in here. A mother knows."

They left me standing at the gate.

I stood there for a long time, hoping they'd change their minds.

They didn't. The person who changed their mind was me. I had traveled all this way for nothing. Where was the next stone for me to overturn? What I needed was a picture of their granddaughter Maria and maybe some context about who she was and how she'd lived. Something I could sink my teeth into and shake until I discovered a motive. Who was the village's biggest gossip, and where could I find her?

Beaten but not defeated, I turned around and trotted down the steep road, avoiding cracks and potholes.

"Psst!"

My head swiveled on its stalk, until I was looking at a large woman with the backend of a poodle mounted to her head. Curls bobbed around her shoulders as she beckoned to me with one finger.

"Me?"

"No, the idiot behind you."

"I heard that," came another voice, this time from my other side. The speaker was a whippet thin woman sweeping her concrete yard with one hand and tapping on a cell phone with the other.

"You were supposed to hear it," the sausage-curled woman

told her. "You, girl, come here." I peered over her gate. She waved her hand at me. "No, no, come in."

I opened the gate and stepped up onto the patio. The sausage-curled woman beamed at me. She had a soft face, a wide mouth, and squinty eyes that said she saw most things and talked about everything. She looked me up and down.

"You were talking to Yiorgos and Maria about Maria and Maria."

I chose my words carefully and limited them to two. "I was."

"And they sent you away?"

Two more words., equally careful. "They did."

Her expression was as sly as a fox's. "You want coffee and maybe a little sweet?"

"I like coffee and sweets," the woman across the street called out. "Hold still. I want to put you both on my Instagram."

The bigger woman shook her fist. "Take your pornography and stick it up your *kolos*."

The neighbor held up her phone. "I think there is a website for that, too."

"Worst enemy?" I asked the sausage-curled woman.

"Elektra is my best friend." She raised her voice. "Come over later and maybe I will let you lick the plates."

Elektra showed her appreciation with a raised middle finger.

The big woman laughed. "Come, come. I am *Kyria* Dora." She steered me indoors and sat me in a room filled with knick knacks and doodads and a million photographs, while I waited for her to return with the promised coffee and sweets. One of the faces in the photographs was familiar. I knew it from a television show I didn't watch and magazines I didn't buy.

"That is my daughter," Kyria Dora said when she came back and noticed me inspecting her family photos.

"Effie Makri from *Greece's Top Hoplite* is your daughter?"

Her face lit up. She had a lot of face. "Do you watch the show?"

Diplomacy time. "Everyone watches *Greece's Top Hoplite*." Everyone except me.

She doled out coffee, cold water, and a crystal dish topped with a mound of sour cherry preserves, while she chatted non-stop about her famous daughter. My stomach's cheering drowned out most of the sound. Restocking my pantry would be my top priority when I got home. *Kyria* Eva had cleaned me out.

Kyria Dora sat across from me. "So, are you going to tell me why were you talking to Yiorgos and Maria about Maria and Maria?"

I didn't know *Kyria* Dora but I knew people just like her. They had different names and faces but they were driven by the same thing: a fresh, exciting story. Information was currency—the grimier the gossip, the higher the denomination. But the thing about the *Kyria* Doras of the world was that information traveled down a two-way street. So I told her who I was and why I'd come to Agria to speak with her neighbors.

When I was done, she stared at me. "You do not know."

"Know what?"

"It was not just their Maria who died on that yacht. It was all of them."

CHAPTER FOURTEEN

"Cousins?"

Kyria Dora's curls bobbed. "Cousins."

Face-palm. Of course.

Multiple Marias. Almost impossible to tell apart. They looked the same because they were the same—almost. Greek naming conventions meant they'd each inherited their first name from the same grandmother. The multiple Maria situation was as Greek as Greek gets.

"Their great-grandmothers," *Kyria* Dora said, "were also named Maria. Great-grandmothers, grandmothers, daughters, granddaughters, a whole family line of Marias. The girls were cousins but not all first cousins, and now they are dead. *Po-po*, what a tragedy." She crossed herself.

In Greece a cousin's cousin's cousin is still a cousin. Sometimes a non-cousin is also a cousin. Don't get me started on the twisted mess of aunts and uncles.

"That poor family," I said.

Kyria Dora's curls bobbed some more. "All those dead girls, and after their daughter Maria went missing, too. *Po-po* ... Some families have bad luck." She asked her next question in a casual tone. "What do you know about Maria? She has been missing for twenty years now. Do you want to know what I think? I think she is dead. Yiorgos and Maria though, they believe she is still alive. What do you think."

"Do you believe in ghosts?"

"I believe in everything, except Macedonians who are not Greek Macedonians. I am the person people come to when they want to remove the *vaskania*, so I believe in many strange things."

Vaskania or the *mati*, also known as the evil eye. Every village has a *Kyria* Dora, an older woman with the power to vanquish the evil eye. The ritual involves a bowl of water, olive oil, and prayer.

I told her about Maria, Harry Vasilikos, the Marias, and their annoying and persistent ghosts. I had nothing to lose. Nobody here knew me except this woman, and she was nodding like she believed me.

"Salt. Of course. There are many things that do not like salt, like my doctor. He is always saying, '*Kyria* Dora, stop drowning all your food in salt, otherwise your body will be pickled when you die,' and '*Kyria* Dora, lose fifty kilos or fifteen years, your choice,' and, '*Kyria* Dora, vinegar cannot heal bones so do not rub it on your neighbor's son when he falls out of a tree and lands on his back.' What does he know? He is a child. Just because he went to a fancy medical school does not mean he knows anything about medicine."

The conversation threatened to be long, winding, and headed in the wrong direction. I threw in a detour that would get her back on the right path.

"What's the problem with salt?"

She sipped her coffee before continuing. "Salt is a purifier and the preserver of life. It is everywhere in the Bible. It keeps away ghosts, demons, and *tsiganes* if you fling it in their eyes."

Tsiganes. A derogatory term for the Romany people living in Greece. Merope didn't have Romanies, but on the mainland they were known for going door-to-door, begging for money. Back in America, the only people who came banging on my parents' door were people who wanted us to find Jesus; Jesus was apparently in their church's garden, sharing fruit with leopards, dinosaurs, and people wearing togas and polo shirts, although not always at the same time.

Kyria Dora had moved on from minerals. "That is a very good story you have told me, so now I will tell you about Yiorgos and Maria's daughter Maria. She was a good girl. People were surprised when she became pregnant with Maria, and without a wedding ring, too. Nobody knows who the father was—maybe not even Maria." Her tiny eyes twinkled, the old witch. "She worked hard to provide for her daughter and be a mother and father to the child. She went back to school in Athens to study and make something of herself." She stopped, eyed me, waited for me to correct her.

"No," I said. "Maria didn't go back to school. Not that I know of, anyway. She joined the workforce."

She clapped once, delighted. "I knew it. Her parents told everybody she was in school, but I did not believe it. What was she?" She leaned closer. "Was she a *putana?* One of those women who takes her clothes off and does a little *tsifteteli* for men? You can tell me."

"She was a stewardess on a yacht."

Kyria Dora's face fell, but not too much. "What is a stewardess? Is that like a *putana?*"

"It's more like a manager, who also does cleaning."

She made a disappointed noise and settled back in her chair. "That does not sound very glamorous or scandalous to me. Whatever she was, and wherever she went, one day she did not come home. Maria was a tiny little doll when it happened. A beautiful child. She always vowed to find her

Mama. She used to say, '*Kyria* Dora, one day Mama and I will be together again.' I hear things. Sometimes people tell me those things, and sometimes people say things when I happen to be under their window listening or standing at their door with a glass." She waved her hand like the eavesdropping was smoke. "Maria and her cousins were close all their lives. They promised when the time came they would help Maria search for her missing mother. And then one day, a month ago, the Marias all left. I know this because her grandmother was crying about how Maria should have just cut off her head and fed it to the chickens because that would be less painful than her leaving."

"Were the Marias all from Agria?"

"No. They were living all over the country. Children do that. They smash their mothers' hearts with an axe, and then they never call, never write, never come home unless you fake chest pains."

I hide a smile behind the demitasse coffee cup. My grandmother also suffered from those same chest pains, until she was forced to upgrade to—as she called it—*mouni* cancer. My parents packed us up and came hurtling across the Atlantic, and then Yiayia conveniently downgraded her vaginal cancer to something sexually transmitted and easily cured with antibiotics.

"What did she look like, Yiorgos and Maria's granddaughter?"

"I do not have a picture ..." Her eyes lit up. "But I know somebody who does." She got up and stuck her head out the window. Her dress hiked up several centimeters, revealing the tops of black knee-high stockings. "*Re,* Elektra? Bring your pornography device over here!"

Kyria Elektra bustled in a moment later, phone in hand. "You want me to Tweet something for you?"

"Look at your photos. Where is Maria Petsini?"

"Which one?"

"Yiorgos and Maria's granddaughter. Hurry up."

"I am looking, I am looking." *Kyria* Dora's friend and neighbor swiped. She held up her phone. A familiar face beamed at me from between a picture of bubbling pastitsio and a purple bathroom. Now, at least, I knew which Maria was which. She was standing between her grandparents, fully clothed and minus the face-concealing sunglasses.

"That is her," *Kyria* Dora crowed. She flicked her hand at her friend in a shooing motion. "You can go now."

Kyria Elektra flipped her off and went back her broom and yard.

"Where did the Marias go when they left?" I asked.

"To Athens. I heard a rumor that a rich man invited them all to travel on his boat. Of course now we all know that rich man was Harry Vasilikos." Her eyebrows waggled. To *Kyria* Dora, travel was a synonym for sex. "Young, beautiful women on a rich man's yacht? I bet they forgot all about finding poor Maria."

I didn't think they forgot at all. Especially not Maria's Maria. The young woman had been lugging that loss on both shoulders since she was tiny.

Cherries went into my mouth. A happy sigh came out. Kyria Dora's smile covered half her face.

"Good?"

"The best."

She shrugged. "They are nothing special."

As I finished up the cherries—which were amazing and she knew it—I mentally sifted information into piles and drew lines between them.

"What do you know about Harry Vasilikos?"

"Harry Vasilikos ..." She picked at a hair on her chin. "Very rich. He never married, you know, which is strange for a Greek man. Probably he is a *poustis*. Everyone seems to be these days. Even my daughter Effie lives with her special friend, who is a woman. It is very fashionable. But we are talking about Harry Vasilikos, yes? Harry has no children. He owns the Royal Pain bread company. You cannot buy his bread here, but you can buy it in Volos."

"Isn't Agria part of Volos?"

Her smile stiffened. "Is Greece part of Turkey? No. Calling Agria part of Volos is the same thing. Yes, Volos likes to pretend Agria is part of the city, and sometimes we let Volos believe Agria is part of the city so that we can take its money. But they are not the same." She patted my hand. "You would not know that because you are not from here. Agria does not sell Harry Vasilikos's bread because his bread is terrible. It comes in slices—slices! How can you rip off chunks of bread if it is already cut into skinny slices? And the flavor ... like eating a *servieta*."

She had just compared Royal Pain bread to a sanitary napkin.

My brain went panning for gold in her words. This information wasn't new but this time it bore a promising shine. "Kyrios Harry never married? Not even once?" Greek men often went from mama to wife. It was either that or buy new socks when they ran out of clean laundry.

"Many rich men collect ex wives, but not Harry Vasilikos."

"What do they say about that?"

Explanations weren't necessary; Kyria Dora knew "they" was every Greek mouth.

"They say he loved a woman once but that she disappeared. Harry never recovered from the loss. He traveled around Greece on his yacht, searching for women who looked like her. Very romantic, but also a little bit pathetic, yes? Who does that?"

Her mouth kept moving but I zoned out. Kyrios Harry had combed Greece for women who resembled his lost love.

Maybe he had found several.

———

Merope was lit up like an aging barfly. A surprise was waiting for me when the ferry lowered the gangway.

Okay, it was Leo, and he was wearing a smile and probably clothes. I only noticed the smile because it was for me. There was no sign of the succubi, but then, like lousy relatives, they only showed up for meals.

"Did you miss me?" I asked him.

"No."

I laughed. "Liar."

Leo's smile evolved into a delicious wolf-like grin. "Sometimes, but apparently I'm bad at it." He lifted my bag off my shoulder and slung it over his own.

"You're carrying my handbag."

He faked a frown. "Do I look pretty?"

"You're the prettiest princess on Merope."

"I try. How was your trip?"

Pieces still didn't fit. Maria's Maria went to hunt for the mother who'd been missing for twenty years. Her cousins had joined the hunt. Harry Vasilikos had loved somebody and lost her, all those years ago. He was constantly searching for women who resembled his dead sweetheart. Then he met the Marias and they joined him on his yacht.

The logical part of my brain said Harry's lost love was Maria Petsini, the woman who kept falling off Merope's highest point.

If she was, then what?

Did Harry Vasilikos push Maria off the cliff two decades ago? Did Maria discover her mother died at the hand—or foot—of *Kyrios* Harry? And if so, did she poison the bread, intending to kill him?

The math didn't work. Why would she kill herself and her cousins in the process? The women were close; *Kyria* Dora had said so.

Maybe the Thessaly Police were running this investigation now, but they'd packed up their toys and scampered back to the mainland. Which left me alone in the sandpit, digging for twenty-year-old fossils. The missing link was here somewhere on Merope. Now I had to find it.

"Boring," I told Leo. "It was a work thing."

"Hunting down an elusive doily again?"

"Never underestimate the allure of the perfect doily."

"Did you find it?"

"Still elusive. The hunt goes on for another day."

Leo squeezed my hand and took me home. He didn't come in and he didn't mention making out. What I got was a kiss on the forehead and a promise that he'd see me tomorrow because he hadn't slept in two days. And I was okay with that because I had lied to him about my trip to the mainland.

In my own defense, the lie was white and necessary. He'd told me to stay out of the Thessaly Police's sandbox.

Me being me, I couldn't. The compulsion to find things was stitched into my soul.

CHAPTER FIFTEEN

MY STOMACH GROWLED. Leo's appearance on the dock had addled my brains and temporarily squelched my hunger—for food, anyway. Now I was home and my appetite was raging. It would have to wait. Arms folded, I paced the living room floor and told my ghosts a bedtime story.

"Once upon a time, there was a pretty brunette in mid-1990s fashions and a Jennifer Aniston hairdo. She met a rich man who considered himself to be good at making money, although his wardrobe really needed work. That whole nautical thing is so late 1970s, by the way," I told *Kyrios* Vasilikos. "She got a job as a stewardess on his yacht so she could afford to raise her small daughter. Then, one day, while the yacht was moored at Merope, the brunette vanished. From that day on, the man traveled the country, looking for his lost love."

Okay, not a good bedtime story. Less Dr. Seuss, more Brothers Grimm—the dark, horrifying original tales, not the newer, brighter retellings.

"What was her name?" I asked *Kyrios* Harry.

He shot his cuffs and stood tall. "Who?"

"The woman you loved, the one who vanished."

The Marias lined up against the couch, every one of them a variation on the same Petsini theme. Maria's daughter was a younger, less angular copy of her mother, but now that I knew what I was looking at, the resemblance was unmistakable.

"What about her?"

"Maria Petsini," I said. "That was her name, wasn't it?"

Kyrios Harry's chin jerked up. "How did you know?"

I pointed to the Marias. "Maria Petsini, Maria Petsini, Maria Petsini, Maria Petsini, and Maria Petsini."

One of the Marias raised her hand. "Maria Andreou."

"Same thing," I said. "You are all cousins."

"Maria's nieces?" Kyrios Harry sounded bewildered. His gaze travelled from face to face.

This time I pointed to Maria's Maria. "Your Maria's daughter."

The ghost of Harry Vasilikos staggered backwards. He fell through the wall, walked out of my bedroom's open door a moment later. "Maria's daughter? I did not know."

"Because we didn't want you to know," the dead woman's equally dead daughter said.

"What was the plan?" I asked her.

She shrugged. "I discovered Mama was last seen on *Kyrios* Harry's boat, so we found a way for him to bring us aboard when he was in Skiathos."

"You all looked like her, so that part wasn't difficult, I bet," I said. "And you were all named Maria.

Maria nodded. "He said we reminded him of someone he cared about," she said.

"Did you poison the bread?"

The Marias exchanged glances. Maria's Maria spoke up. "It wasn't me. It wasn't any of us. We didn't want *Kyrios* Harry or anyone to die. I just wanted to find Mama."

"What was your plan, once you boarded his yacht?"

She looked at *Kyrios* Harry, who was still processing the shock. "To earn his trust and ask him about my mama. Then follow the trail from there."

"But you didn't have time," I said. Not a question but a simple fact. Time had run out for everyone. As soon as they'd boarded the Royal Pain with that bread in the galley, their clock had stopped ticking.

"I did not hurt your mother," *Kyrios* Harry told Maria. "I loved her even though she never knew. I never stopped looking for her."

"She didn't know?" I asked him.

"No." His smile was a tiny, humorless smear. "Even twenty years ago I was too old for her. What did I have to offer an attractive young woman besides money? Nothing. She was better than that."

Maybe, I thought, so was he. "What happened before she disappeared?"

He shrugged. "I have asked myself the same question a million times or more. When I sail, I replay that day over and over in my head. Nothing changes. No answers come. The day was a normal one on Merope. I played *tavli* at the *kafeneio*, I argued about politics with old friends and acquaintances."

Playing backgammon and drinking coffee was a favorite pastime for Greek men of a certain age.

"And Maria Petsini?"

"That day she went off exploring on her own. She did not like those two *malakes*, Yiorgos and Dimitri."

"Triantafillou?"

"Who else?"

"Why not?"

"Because they are cheap and she did not like that they refused to pay their employees what they were worth. They thought I was a fool for paying fair wages when I could have saved money paying less. She got angry with them and would not breathe the same air as they did, after that."

Nothing had changed. The brothers were still short-changing their employees according to Stephanie Dola.

"So you last saw her the morning she disappeared, then you spent the day with the Triantafillou brothers?"

"Yes."

"What did you do when you realized Maria was missing?"

"I talked to the police, I talked to people on the island. Everybody had a different story. Some said they saw her boarding the ferry to Skiathos. Others said she went to Mykonos. The police would not do anything because to them she was not missing—she left. I traveled to both islands, again and again, but nobody had seen her."

I believed him. Maria's face said she did, too. But I still had questions.

"Why bring the Marias aboard your yacht?"

His eyes reddened. "When a woman's heart breaks she tells the world. When a man's heart breaks, it breaks quietly, along with the rest of him. After Maria disappeared, I turned to my business. I never stopped turning to my business, even to touch other women. Then, when I saw the Marias, I could not believe how much they looked like the woman I had lost. I could not resist asking them to travel with me for a while, to keep an old man company. But they were never her. All I could do was look and imagine what might have been."

I sat on my office chair, tried to think. I looked up at their grim, transparent faces.

"Help me," I said. "I have all these dead people and no killers."

We exchanged helpless glances, *Kyrios* Harry, the Marias, and me.

"If I knew I would tell you," *Kyrios* Harry said, "and they would, too."

The chorus line of Marias agreed.

My stomach growled. There wasn't going to be any serious thinking happening on an empty stomach. *Kyria* Dora's cherries were ancient history, and I hadn't eaten since.

I got up and went to the kitchen. "I need a sandwich. My brain requires fuel."

No sandwich for me. Like Old Mother Hubbard, my cupboards were bare. Condiments I had, but unless I wanted ketchup soup with a lightly toasted napkin, I would have to go shopping.

"Give me ten minutes." I grabbed my keys, phone, purse. "While I'm gone, I need you all to think. Who could have poisoned the bread? Who would want you dead? Names and reasons."

My phone rang.

"Can you babysit?" Toula sounded desperate. "We're in the middle of dinner and the babysitter just called, threatening to run away."

"Why?"

"Can you look after Milos and Patra or not?"

Me, Dog Fart, Pinkie Pie, and a pile of sandwiches? As far as ideas went it didn't suck.

"Sure."

"Great."

Without another word, she hung up. There was scuffling outside my door, then a knock. I opened the door to find a scrawny teenage girl with two nose rings and a T-shirt that read *Fack This, Fack That, Fack Everything.* Her makeup was black and smeared in circles around her eyes. I suspected it was deliberate. Milos and Patra was hovering either side of the teenage ray of sunshine, chins on their chests, miserable. I remembered the babysitter when she was a cute kid in pastels and ponytails, before she got hit with the teenage hormones and went all Marilyn Manson.

"You need a proofreader," I said.

"Fack you," she said in what I decided was supposed to be English. It was hard to tell with the typo in her words. "Take them. *Kyria* Toula said you would."

"*Kyria* Toula says a lot of things," I called out as she stalked off, presumably to punch herself in the eyes again. I stuffed my things into my bag. "I hope you two can handle a walk, because that's what we're doing. Are you hungry?

"Again?" Milos whined.

"You sure like to walk a lot," Patra said. "Are you worried about getting fat?"

I stepped in between them and held their hands. Better to divide and conquer ahead of time. "Tonight, I'm worried about starvation. I need food. It's this or Crusty Dimitri's, and I like you both too much to feed you Crusty Dimitri's food."

Milos looked up at me. "What does 'fack' mean?"

"It's something your mother has done at least twice, so you should ask her."

My stomach protested all the way to the More Super Market. The tiny market's lights were off. The door was locked. No sandwiches for us.

I was about to walk away when I spotted the Triantafillos brothers' three-wheeled Motoemil truck parked in the narrow alley between their shop and its neighbor. Motoemil quit making the three-wheeler in the early seventies. Motoemil also quit being Motoemil in the 1980s. Nowadays the company made boat trailers and called itself Emilios Trailers.

"They are up to no good," a voice said in my ear. "Trust me, they are making trouble."

I jumped. Vasilis Moustakas and his walker had materialized alongside me. As always, the dead man was wearing pajamas with a strategic opening.

"Stay right there. Don't move," I told my niece and nephew.

"Do you need to fart?" Patra asked, wide-eyed. "That's what Mama does when she needs to fart."

Virgin Mary, these children. "No, I just need to make a phone call."

I moved far enough that they couldn't overhear me easily but stayed close enough that I could tackle them if they tried to make a run for it.

I spoke into my phone. "What kind of trouble?"

"I fucked your *yiayia*," *Kyrios* Moustakas said.

Eye roll. "You and everyone else."

"They took something that does not belong to them."

"Who? The Triantafillou brothers?"

Kyrios Moustakas and his walker shuffled away.

The Triantafillou brothers were tight but they weren't criminals. Not unless frugality, underpaying their employees, and leaving goods on their shelves decades past the Use By Date were crimes. So what was the old man talking about?

I cupped my hands against the glass door and peered inside. Not easy. Stephanie Dola wasn't paid enough to wipe a cloth over the glass.

Squint.

Sure enough, the decrepit brothers were inside, loading something onto their shelves from a pallet.

Bread. Royal Pain bread. The Royal Pain bread someone had poisoned.

I hammered on the door. "Stop!"

The brothers looked up. Leaning heavily on his walking stick, Dimitri ambled over to the door.

"The bread," I said through the glass. "It's poisoned. You can't sell it, remember?"

With his hand, he pushed his fleshy earlobe forward.

I jabbed my finger at the door handle. "Open the door."

He nodded. His liver-spotted hand shook as he went hunting through a hundred or so keys on a massive keyring. Hours later—or minutes—he found the right key, pushed the door open.

I almost fell into the shop, pulling my sister's kids behind me. "I thought the police confiscated the Royal Pain bread. There's a chance it's poisoned."

"It is not poisoned," Kyrios Yiorgos said. He was stacking bread on the shelf.

"Did they test it already? That was fast." Leo hadn't said a word about the bread when he'd picked me up at the dock.

"This is from the mainland. It came earlier today, direct from the factory. No poison."

Relief washed over me. Good. Great. No one else was dying anytime soon, unless it was from natural causes or the result of bickering with their neighbor over wandering farm animals.

"I meant to come earlier but I was on the mainland. I haven't eaten anything except cherries all day. Can I still buy something?"

"Of course!" He stopped stacking. "Whatever you want, Dimitri will ring it up for you."

Kyrios Dimitri took Stephanie's place behind the counter. Groans leaked out of his mouth as he eased himself onto the stool. "My feet," he said. "All winter they hurt. This year is going to be the coldest in history."

I selected a jar of Merenda. Not my first sandwich of choice tonight, but the deli was closed up and all the meats and cheeses had been banished to the refrigerator. Neither Triantafillou brother looked like they'd survive cutting cheese, so I made do with the hazelnut spread.

"You like Merenda, yes?" I asked Milos and Patra.

"Mama only lets us have it on weekends," Milos told me solemnly.

"Mama isn't here." I looked around to make sure I wasn't lying to my own flesh and blood. "If you don't tell her, I won't tell her unless she tortures me. If that happens, you're on your own."

Milos looked at his sister. "Will you tell Mama?"

"Only if she asks me."

Good enough. I carried the jar to the checkout.

Kyrios Dimitri picked up the hazelnut spread. "You have bread to go with that?"

My face fell. "No." *Kyria* Eva had taken everything except condiments.

"Lucky for you we have bread now," he said.

Kyrios Yiorgos quit stacking long enough to throw me a loaf of Royal Pain bread. "For you it is free."

"Really? You're sure this isn't poisoned?"

He shook his head, laughing. "No poison. For that we would charge you extra."

Triantafillou brothers giving away free bread? Obviously my lucky night. They never gave away anything.

I paid for the Merenda and wrangled my niece and nephew, not caring that the brothers' generosity didn't extend to giving me a plastic bag. Free was free, and the Triantafillou brother never gave away something they could sell.

"Who was that man in the pajamas and why were you pretending to talk into your phone?" Patra asked me.

Full stop. Jaw drop. "Man?"

"The naughty man," she said.

I crouched down in front of her. "Why was he naughty?"

"Because he was peeing all over the road."

"You saw him peeing?"

Milos poked his sister. "He wasn't peeing, he just had his thing out like he was going to pee."

Thoughts were whizzing around my head. It was a spin cycle in there. "Wait—you both saw a man?"

"You saw him, too, *Thea* Allie," Patra said. "You were talking to him."

Slowly, I unfurled my body until I was standing. I blew out a long sigh.

"You're right, I did see him and I did talk to him."

Patra giggled. "He was like a window. That was funny."

"Like an old man window," her brother said.

"Let's go," I said.

"You're not angry?"

"Angry? Why would I be angry?"

"Mama gets angry when we see people she can't see."

"How many have you seen?"

"They're everywhere," they said together.

———

Kyrios Harry eyed the loaf in my hand. "Is that my bread?"

"No. It's my bread. My free bread." I quickly slapped together three sandwiches, spreading the chocolate-hazelnut goop thick. Then I made a fourth one because my stomach told me one wouldn't be enough, and even two wasn't likely to make a dent in my hunger. I carried the sandwiches to the living room. Milos and Patra were hanging out with four of the Marias. The dead women laughed as Toula's kids took turns throwing things through them. Then Dead Cat showed up and Patra fell in love. Now that the Merenda sandwiches were a reality instead of a fantasy, their interest in eating had waned.

No problem. More for me. I carried them to the couch.

"Did you figure out who murdered you yet?" I asked *Kyrios* Harry and Maria's Maria.

"We don't know," Maria said.

I bit into the sandwich. The woman from Agria, Kyria Dora, was right. Royal Pain bread did taste like a sanitary napkin. Not that I'd eaten a sanitary napkin since I was a toddler, and even then it was a small bite. The paper taste didn't slow me down. I took another bite, followed by another.

"Today is my lucky day," I said. "Some might even say it's historic. Do you know why?" I didn't wait for an answer. "Because for the first time ever, the Triantafillou brothers gave something away. For free. No money at all."

I was four bites into the sandwich. It wasn't bad but it was dinner.

"The Triantafillou brothers? Yiorgos and Dimitri?" Kyrios Harry asked.

Chewing, I nodded.

He snorted. "Those two *malakes*. They wanted to buy my company for donkey *archidia*, and now they are giving my bread away."

Huh. Interesting. The brothers wanted to buy it for balls, which apparently weren't worth much. The way men usually acted you'd think they were gold. "They wanted to buy Royal Pain?"

"For nothing. For *skata*."

"When?"

"Last month they made an offer. I told them to *gamisou*."

My gaze slid sideways. Toula's kids hadn't noticed his suggestion that the Triantafillou brothers go screw themselves.

"How did they take it?"

"They said they were going to destroy Royal Pain."

The Triantafillou brothers were greedy and they had managed to downgrade thrift from a virtue to a sin, but I'd never heard a whisper of a vindictive streak running through the Triantafillou family. They seemed content to be kings of all the groceries they surveyed.

"But you made a deal for them to sell your bread here, yes?"

"No. There was no deal. Not yet. I do not understand how they are selling my bread when there is no deal."

I stopped chewing. "When they said they were going to destroy Royal Pain, was that a joking thing between men? A friendly threat?"

"Yiorgos and Dimitri Triantafillou have not been my friends for many years."

Neurons fired in my head. "Would you say ... twenty years?" I said, mouth full of sandwich. My mother's voice told me not to talk with my mouth full. Good thing my mother was on a ship, thousands of kilometers from here.

"About that long, sure."

"What happened?"

"We fought."

"Over Maria?"

"Maria, yes. The Triantafillous expected me to control my employee."

"Why?"

"Like I told you earlier, she did not like the way they treated their employees. She was vocal about it. And I did not like the way they expected me to discipline her for having thoughts and principles—principles I share. I know what people say about me, but they never say I am cheap. I always pay those who work for me a fair wage. She ran away and disappeared before I could tell her that I agreed with her."

"No." A searing knife cut across my stomach. "She didn't run away."

Then I vomited on the floor.

CHAPTER SIXTEEN

LEO DIDN'T PICK UP. His phone went to voicemail. Between retches, I left him a message. Merope wasn't exactly the crime capital of the world. Most nights the police went home to their beds, relatively sure they could get a full night's sleep. Leo had told me he was going to bed, so I staggered into the hallway, gripping the leftover loaf of Royal Pain bread and three and half sandwiches.

Jimmy Kontos was sitting on the steps. His hair and beard were speckled with bits of greenery. Someone had been hiding in the bushes again.

"She went out. Again. She goes out a lot."

Like I cared about Lydia and her whereabouts right now. Too busy dying.

"Is Leo home?"

"Why? You looking to get some?" He got up and squinted at me. "Hey, you don't look so good."

The hallway tilted, or maybe it was me. "Leo? Where is he?"

"He went to the store."

"Which store?"

He shrugged. "One of them. Why?"

"Which one?"

"The More Super Market. He went to get Merenda because I ate the last of it. You people know there's nothing Super or More Super about that place, yes?"

I slapped my phone into his hand. "My sister's kids are inside my apartment. Call Toula to come and get them. She's in my Contacts. Can you do that?"

"Is that the same Toula who used to give Leo—"

"Don't you dare finish that sentence. Just call her."

"Sure. Okay. You really don't look good."

"I'm allergic to dwarves," I told him.

I stumbled down the stairs. A haze clouded my vision. Things weren't looking good or clear. My future shrunk to the approximate length of a banana. I threw my leg over my bicycle, missed, tried easing it over, and set off for the More Super Market.

Late. No traffic. Not this time of year. No one saw me when I stopped to throw up in a gutter. There was nothing left inside me except—for some inexplicable reason—carrots. That didn't stop the pain grinding lower. Back on the bicycle, I wobbled toward the store, hoping to find Leo.

At the More Super Market, the three-wheeler was still parked outside. So was Leo's car. My bicycle fell against the wall. I staggered to the glass door and grabbed the handle.

Locked.

My fists were weak hammers. Really, they were rubber whack-a-mole mallets. Soft and ultimately useless. Why had I eaten that stupid bread? The Triantafillou brothers didn't do philanthropy. I should have realized they would never give away something without expecting something.

The something they were expecting was my death.

But why? I was nobody.

On the other side of the door, a shadow moved. It aimed a rictus grin at me. The door opened.

"*Kaloste*," Yiorgos Triantafillou said. "My brother and I were having a party with a friend of yours. He came looking for Merenda and so we offered him a free meal."

Sure enough, Leo was sitting behind the counter with *Kyrios* Dimitri. The counter was covered with food. Cheese. Meats. An open jar of Merenda. A stack of Royal Pain slices. Leo was eating his way through the pile. The succubi were there, watching him fork feta into his mouth. No bleeding. No choking. They were sighing happily and enjoying the view.

"Allie?" Leo said. "What are you doing?"

"Stop," I said. The word sounded smudged. "The bread."

Leo's features blurred. Was he frowning?

I sagged against the counter. "The bread is poisoned. The bread is poisoned and they know it. They killed Harry Vasilikos and the Marias, and they killed Maria Petsini. Virgin Mary, I'm starting to think all the old people on this island are murderers." Nausea squeezed my stomach. I dry-heaved.

"Who is Maria Petsini?" Leo asked. He looked taller now. Was he standing? Something was in his hand. I couldn't make it out. Phone. Maybe gun.

Yiorgos Triantafillou held his hands out, palms up. "They were accidents."

I wiped my sleeve across my mouth. "Accidents?"

"We never meant for anyone to die. They were just supposed to get sick and ruin Royal Pain when the news got out that people were getting sick from the bread. He refused to sell the company to us, and we really wanted that company. The bread is made so cheaply that it is a money-making machine."

"But they did die," I said.

"We never thought Harry would serve his own bread on his yacht, or eat it himself. Royal Pain bread is *skata*."

"It is *skata*," *Kyrios* Dimitri said.

"But you were here on Merope all this time," I said. "How did you poison the bread?

"There are always people willing to do a thing for money, even when that thing is crime," *Kyrios* Yiorgos said.

"They do ask for more money when it is a crime," his brother said.

Kyrios Yiorgos made a constipated face. "Too much money. Ten, twenty years ago, we could have saved ourselves the money and poisoned the bread ourselves. Now, we are too old. Who has the energy for crimes?"

Their faces were fuzzy now. "What about Maria Petsini?" I prompted them.

The Triantafillou brothers were on the move. Leo was herding them, arm outstretched. Gun. Not his phone. *Kyrios* Yiorgos opened a bag of bread. He offered it to his brother, then took a slice for himself.

"Another accident," Kyrios Yiorgos said. He stuffed the bread into his mouth and reached for more.

I braced my back against the counter. Leo had them pinned against the shelves of bread. "Twenty years ago, you pushed her off the cliff," I said. "How is that an accident?"

"She made us angry and we pushed her," *Kyrios* Yiorgos said.

"Angry?"

"She interfered in our business, and we do not like people interfering in our business."

What motivated the Triantafillou brothers to do anything? Money. "Maria Petsini cost you money somehow?"

"That *malakas* Harry Vasilikos brought her to Merope on his yacht. She worked for him, did you know? But he was in love with her, so he let her open her mouth and talk. Talk, talk, talk. All that woman did was talk."

"To our employees," *Kyrios* Dimitri said.

A picture was starting to form. A blurry picture. At the same time, I was starting to fade. I glanced sideways at Leo; he'd eaten the bread, too. We were going to die together. Every bit as unromantic as those two nitwits, Romeo and Juliet.

"She used a word we did not like," *Kyrios* Yiorgos said. "Union."

His brother nodded. "That woman said we were not paying our employees what was fair. She said we did not give them proper vacation time and decent hours. We told her this is Greece, where people enjoy working hard because they have families to provide for. She said nobody could provide for a family on what we paid."

"And Harry encouraged her. He liked that she spoke her mind. Who likes a woman who speaks her mind? Nobody, that is who. And a woman who was only his employee? *Po-po* ..."

Welcome to Greece, where it was often still 1840.

"Harry was in love with the woman but she was not in love with him," *Kyrios* Yiorgos said. "She was more interested in things like work and money and saving—for what, she never did say and we did not care. One night we asked her to meet us so we could discuss this union idea. When she arrived, we drove her up the hill."

"Where you pushed her," I said.

"Only a little nudge," *Kyrios* Yiorgos said.

Kyrios Dimitri nodded. "The falling part was her own fault."

The brothers were frugal, even when it came to murder. "How did you explain her disappearance to Harry Vasilikos?"

They looked at each other. "Explain it? We did not explain anything. Merope did everything for us. Gossip, rumors, all the talk made Maria Petsini disappear—*poof!* like magic. One person saw her boarding the ferry to Mykonos, another saw her sailing to the mainland. Some swore she sailed into the sunset with a rich man who was not Harry Vasilikos."

"Merope takes care of its own," Dimitri Triantafillou said. He ate another slice of Royal Pain's bread-shaped maxi-pad.

"We call that murder," Leo said. "You're both going to prison."

The brothers were aghast. "But we already told you, we only nudged her."

"The bread," I muttered. Speech was harder now.

"We already told you, someone else poisoned the bread," Kyrios Yiorgos said. "How can we go to prison for murders we did not do?"

"If you didn't poison the bread on the yacht, who did?" Leo asked.

Oh, oh, oh. Even my fog addled brain knew this one. "Eva Vasiliko."

Leo's features smudged more. "Why?"

"Because Johnny Margas told her to," I said. "Their hired hand was Yiannis Margas."

"Johnny, Harry, we are all the same shit," Dimitri Triantafillou said. "And Johnny was worse than most. He would do anything for a drachma."

We had euros now, but I didn't correct him. I couldn't. The Royal Pain bread was cutting my insides to ribbons.

"Why did he do it?" Leo asked. Was it me or was he more pale now?

"I know this one, too." Pain slashed my midsection. I doubled over, arms around my middle, and looked up at Leo, who now had two faces Picasso would be proud of. "Two reasons. Johnny planned to get rid of his wife and hitch his donkey to Angela Zouboulaki. She owns Royal Pain's closest competition, although she didn't know until this week. With his wife dead and Angela in his bed, he would have his greasy fingers in two major bread companies. Lucky for Angela she discovered Johnny lied about his age ... by twenty years. And Johnny was looking for an excuse to stick it to Harry Vasilikos. Years ago, Harry Vasilikos offered him a job Johnny thought was beneath him. I guess he's been carrying a grudge all this time."

The Triantafillou brothers were stuffing bread into their mouths faster now.

"Stop them," I said. "I'm going to be seriously annoyed if they die before they do prison time."

Leo groaned, long and pained. Fell to his knees. From there it was a short tumble, so his face wouldn't be too banged up if he survived—*if*. Somebody was crying. My face was wet so it was definitely me.

The succubi crouched beside him. "Dying," Bleeder said.

"Definitely dying," Choker agreed. "We have seen it before. We will see it again."

"And again."

"Don't you dare die on me." I fell on my knees beside him. "I can't do this. Not again." My fingers found his phone and Constable Pappas's number.

"Send everyone you've got to the More Super Market." The phone clanked on the floor. I didn't have it in me to end the call.

There was a loud, ripping BOOM like a small bomb exploding. The stink of sewage filled the shop.

Yiorgos Triantafillou groaned. "I think I *kaka'd* in my *sovraka*."

Not me and not my underwear. Thank the Virgin Mary.

CHAPTER SEVENTEEN

THE TRIANTAFILLOU BROTHERS were good at murder but they sucked at suicide. Their poisoned bread had killed a boatload of people. Stuffing themselves with the same bread gave them the intestinal equivalent of norovirus, E. coli, and salmonella, all rolled up into one explosive nightmare.

I wasn't there to see or smell it. Nor was I there when the police from Thessaly marched in and took custody of the brothers. They wound up in a cell with Johnny Margas, who discovered slicing twenty years off his age in prison wasn't a stellar idea.

Everyone else was still dead, including *Kyria* Hondrou's chickens. Apparently the Triantafillou brothers had needed test subjects, so they loaded up their three-wheeler and delivered a pile of bread to the Hondrou farm. Like most people, *Kyria* Hondrou got giddy over free stuff. End result: dead chickens.

Leo and I almost joined the dead.

Almost.

What saved us was eating in moderation. Who knew nutritionists and doctors were right? Eating in moderation won us a two-night, all expenses paid stay in Merope's hospital. One room. Two beds.

Sleeping was impossible. For me, anyway. Ghosts roamed the halls, night and day, complaining about hospital food.

Toula came. She cried a lot at my bedside. More than once, I caught her staring at Leo across the room. Who could blame her? He was nice to look at. She lectured me about the dangers of eating processed food, which Royal Pain bread clearly was. Then she hugged my neck until I couldn't breathe and made me promise to never die.

When our two nights were up, Leo drove us home. We didn't talk; there was too much to say.

Harry Vasilikos and the Marias were waiting.

"It's over," I told them. "Yiorgos and Dimitri Triantafillou had Johnny Margas poison the bread. He outsourced to his wife." I looked at the Maria who had lost her mother. Too bad I couldn't hug her. Her face said she was in dire need of one. "Yiorgos and Dimitri Triantafillou was responsible for your mother's death. She died trying to be a decent human being."

She sat on my couch and cried.

Hugging her was impossible, but I could give her closure.

"Do you want to see her?"

Maria jerked her head up. *Kyrios* Harry tensed. Hope radiated from their faces. "Is she here?" she asked.

"Come with me."

I walked them to the top of Merope, where we watched Maria Petsini fall. Like always, she reappeared, face turned to the sea.

Her daughter stepped forward. She seemed younger now than ever. "Mama?"

Maria looked up from the white swirl, her expression curious. "I know you."

"It's Maria, Mama. It's time to go."

I looked at *Kyrios* Harry. "Are you going to speak to her?"

He tilted his chin up-down. "No. I love her, but she never loved me."

"Are you okay?"

"Maria is dead but she is still in the world, and that makes today a good one." He turned to me. "I made you a promise, eh?"

"You did." I bit back tears. "Tell me."

"Andreas spoke to me. He said to tell you he never would have left you if there was any other choice."

"Is he okay?"

"He will be, when he knows you are at peace. Andreas works in the Afterlife's waiting room now, helping the newly dead cope with their situation when they are struggling to understand what has happened. He helped me. At first, I did not want to believe I was dead."

My laugh was damp. "That sounds like Andreas. He was a therapist."

Hypertrophic cardiomyopathy lead to sudden cardiac death that night in the Super Super Market. He never knew —we never knew—that parts of his heart were thickening, conspiring against our future. His death came out of nowhere, without warning.

"He never came to see me. Why?"

"If you pick at a wound it never heals." He touched my shoulder. It felt like the sea's fog. "You were loved, and you will be loved again. Soon, I think." *Kyrios* Harry closed his eyes. "How do I do this, how do I leave?"

"You have to want to go."

There was a soft *poof!*, like the popping of a bubble, and Harry Vasilikos vanished. Maria Petsini and the Marias followed not long after. Finally, I was alone on the cliff, with the cold Aegean Sea in front of me and the village at my back. No ghosts. No nothing.

Inner peace came and went. My niece and nephew popped into my head. Like me, they could see ghosts.

I called Toula.

"Why did you go to see Leo? Tell me the truth. I need to know."

She sighed. "I don't want to talk about this."

"Milos and Patra, they saw something didn't they?"

"They saw something—something bad."

"Was it a ghost? It was a ghost, wasn't it?"

"My children are crazy," she said. "Probably they have been eating lead paint. It's all over the island, you know."

I wasn't crazy and I had never eaten lead paint, as far as I knew. "What does Leo have to do with lead paint?"

More sighing, deep and angsty. "Last week, I took them to the playground, to get some fresh air before the weather turns too cold. They were playing when suddenly they started screaming that they had killed a boy."

"Killed him how?"

"They said he challenged them to see who could go higher on the swings—"

"Let me guess: he went higher, his swing spun over the top, and he hit the ground with a nauseating splat. Then Milos and Patra freaked out because they thought the accident was their fault."

There was silence. Lots of it, while Toula's wheels turned. Then: "How did you know?"

"The boy's name was Raymond Webber. He died in a freak swing accident when he was visiting Merope with his parents during the 1970s. The swings were different then. After his accident, the swings were swapped out for swings that didn't flip. Raymond really likes the playground and doesn't want to move on. In a way, he's Merope's own Peter Pan. You went to see Leo, but when you got there all you had was a story and no body to with it. That's why you choked and left before spitting out the story. On a scale of one to ten, how close am I?"

More silence. Too much of it.

"Toula?"

I looked at my phone. How long had I been talking to myself? Under stress, Toula detached and, apparently, ended calls. No problem. She needed time to process. And when she had questions I would be here—for her and the kids.

What now?

Detective Leo Samaras, that's what. I heard the low rumble of his engine, climbing the steep hill, the abrupt silence as he turned the key. Then I heard his voice, calling my name.

"I saw you walking up here. You okay?" He planted himself beside me. The gap between us was narrow and I could feel his body heat. He took my hand and shoved it into his coat pocket, enveloped in his. For this moment, everything was quiet and completely normal. No ghosts. No demons. No sisters who may or may not be harboring a crush on an ex and dealing with two unexpectedly unusual kids. No one trying to kill me. That last thing was the best. Attempted murder is hell on the self-esteem.

"Totally okay."

Deadpan: "You hungry?"

I laughed. "No more food. Ever. Especially bread."

"I wasn't talking about food." He turned to face me, brushed back the hair that had escaped from my ponytail. His eyes were dark and serious—seriously dirty.

Yowza. "Oh."

"I like you—a lot."

"I see dead people."

"And sometimes I leave my wet towel on the bedroom floor. It's there right now."

"That's bad. It might be a deal-breaker." The cold wind took another stab at me. I shivered.

The hand that was in my hair found my waist. He reeled me in until I was tucked under his chin. "Warmer?"

"My *kolos* is still cold."

"Come home with me and I'll warm it up. By the time I'm done with you, you'll be sweating."

"I might even want food after."

"I have food."

"I'll need cake," I said. "You want cake?"

"I like cake."

"Everyone likes cake." I pulled away. "What are you waiting for?"

We drove down to the village. Five minutes later we were standing outside the Cake Emporium. Halloween was over. The decorations were gone. They'd been replaced with sugar skulls and candles in a million bright, cheerful colors.

"They're beautiful," I breathed. And they were. Betty Honeychurch did decorating like it was her religion.

"What's beautiful?" Leo's reflection joined mine in the Cake Emporium's window.

"The window display."

He shook his head. "What are you talking about?"

"The Cake Emporium." I pointed to the sign, gently swaying from the sea's cool push.

"Allie," Leo said. "There's nothing there."

Thank you for reading *Royal Ghouls,* the second Greek Ghouls mystery.

Want to be notified when my next book is released? Sign up for my mailing list: http://eepurl.com/ZSeuL. Or like my Facebook page at: https://www.facebook.-com/alexkingbooks.

All reviews are appreciated. You may help another reader fall in love ... or avoid a terrible mistake.

All my best,
　　Alex A. King

ALSO BY ALEX A. KING

Printed in Great Britain
by Amazon

76709240R00147